THE THUG IS MINE

BY:

NATIONAL BESTSELLING AUTHORS,

TYANNA & MZ. BIGGS

Published by Tyanna Presents
&
Biggs Publishing Group, LLC.

Author's Note:

Please take the time to leave an honest review on either Amazon or Goodreads after reading the book. Your support is greatly appreciated. Also, feel free to reach out to us anytime via the contact information listed below. Happy Reading... ☺

~Mz. Biggs & Author Tyanna

Want to connect with us? Here's how:

Mz. Biggs:

Email: authoress.mz.biggs@gmail.com

Twitter: @mz_biggz

Instagram: mz.biggs

Goodreads: Mz. Biggs

Facebook: https://www.facebook.com/authoress.biggs

Author Page: https://www.facebook.com/MzBiggs3/

Look for Mz. Biggs' Reading Group on Facebook:

Lounging with Mz. Biggs

Tyanna:

Email: 35tyanna.coston@gmail.com

Email: tyannapresents1@gmail.com

Facebook: @Tyanna Coston

Instagram: @author_tyanna2016

Look for Tyanna's Reading Group on Facebook:

TP Book Paradise

Strung Out On His Dope Loving (Standalone)

A Hip Hop Love in South Jersey (Standalone)

Rose and Thorne: A Fairytale in the Hood (Standalone)

Make-up Won't Cover the pain: Domestic Violence

(Anthology)

Hood Lovin: Santa Sent Me a Hood Legend (Standalone)

Confessing My Love To A Hustler (Standalone)

Melani: A BBW Love On The Rise (Part: 1-2)

Magic City: Capturing a Bosses Heart (Part: 1-2)

Big Girls Love Dope Boys Too (Anthology)

Married to the Community D (Part: 1-2)

Downgraded: From Wifey to Mistress (Part: 1-3)

A Mother's Prayer (Part: 1-2)

Heart of A Champion... Mind of A Killer (Standalone)

Turned Out by My Husband's Best Man (Standalone)

Ain't No Lovin' Like Gulf Coast Lovin' On The 4th of July (A Novella)

This Is Why I Love You (A Novella)

The Hood Was My Claim to Fame (A Novella)

A Killer Valentine's (Anthology)

Bouncing Back After Zaddy Gave Me the Clap (Standalone)

Tantalizing Temptations in New Orleans (An Erotic Novella)

Santa Blessed Me with a Jacktown Boss (Novella)

Diamonds and Pearls (Standalone)

Dating A Female Goon (Standalone/Collaboration)

Pregnant by My Best Friend's Husband (Part: 1-2)

Wifed Up by A Down South Boss (Thug Love Collection/Anthology)

Creepin' With the Plug Next Door (Part: 1-3)

Creepin' With My Co-Worker (Part 1)

Crushin' On A Dope Boy: Cashae and Tay (Anthology)

The Autobiography of A Boss's Wife (Collaboration)

Scorned by The Love of A Thug (Standalone)

Synopsis:

National Bestselling Authors of In Love with My Cuddy Buddy and From Cuddy Buddy to Wifey, Tyanna Coston and Mz. Biggs are back with another jaw dropping read as you meet Zion, Amara, Majestic, and Majesty.

Zion didn't have the best life growing up. Living with his girlfriend of 3 years and their two children, he was determined to give them the life he never had. Hitting the streets, he didn't mind starting from the bottom and putting himself in position to where he and his family wanted for nothing. Met with a lot of complications along the way, he is ready for a change. That means putting some people out of his life and allowing others to enter. He learns the hard way that family doesn't mean anything when you have to question their loyalty.

Three years with Zion was more than enough time for Amara to realize she wanted more. She loved her children but not enough to continue to live in what she considered to be poverty. Zion hadn't been the only man in her life for a while and she was ready to let him go. She made up in her mind that she was going to give him a few more months to start making the moves she wanted him to make to give her the lifestyle she desired, or it was over forever. Being caught up in her own indiscretions, she has no choice but to learn the meaning of the saying, "All that glitters isn't gold."

Money has always been the main priority for Majestic. That was until he allowed Amara and Majesty to enter his heart. Always having a hustler's mentality, he is stunned to constantly find himself in situations that could lead his empire to disaster all thanks to Amara. Majesty was his sister. Being in her life and making sure she was good was a top priority for him. However, being able to find a common ground between Amara and Majesty ends up being more trouble than it's worth. Love starts to lead him down a dangerous path when he lands in a situation that he won't be able to control. Who will stick by him through it all?

Majesty was Majestic's twin. They weren't close growing up, but she knew she could always count on him. When one night changed her life, she had to pick up and start over. The only person she could lean on was Majestic. That was until one chance encounter bought her face to face with Zion. Getting to know him adds the excitement she always wanted and needed in her life. Little did she know, they were connected in more ways than one.

Faced with many challenges, Zion, Amara, Majestic, and Majesty have to decide what choices will lead them to happiness. A mixture of love, lust, greed, and betrayal will have you on the edge of your seat as you tune in to this blazing new African American Urban Fiction series, The Thug Is Mine.

Chapter One:

Zion

Glancing down at the radio on my 2012 Toyota Camry, I couldn't believe that the time read 8:44 pm. It was the second day I'd been away from home. My girlfriend, Amara had been blowing me up. Knowing how she was, I really felt like getting a hotel for the night. I was too tired to stay up arguing with her.

Ring... Ring... Ring...

The phone rung for the umpteenth time. I deliberated over whether I wanted to answer it or not. It was Amara's ass calling again.

"Yo?" I finally answered the phone and said.

"Yo? What the fuck you mean, yo? Where are you, Zion?" she quizzed.

"I'm on my way to the house now," I replied.

"Now? Nigga, you've been gone a whole two days on some "single" shit and now you expect to come in here like ain't shit happen?" she fussed.

"Look Ma, I know I've been gone. But, it's not like you don't know where the hell I've been. We got bills to pay and you not out here trying to work anywhere to help out."

"Why should I have to work? I wasn't working when you met me. Besides, you said you were going to take care of me," she whined. I knew that was her way of trying to get over on me. Whenever we would get into it or she wanted something, she would start whining because she knew that shit made me weak.

"Cut the bullshit, Amara. I said I was going to take care of you as in I was going to make sure the bills were paid and that your stomach was full of food and my seeds. That didn't mean your ass shouldn't work. Hell, it's not like you cook or clean," I chided.

"Neither does Cardi B., but she still got a ring," she remarked. I could hear her ruthless ass giggling in the background, but the shit wasn't funny to me.

"She also got cheated on numerous times, so I wouldn't be too quick to compare myself to her," I returned.

"What are you trying to say?"

"Exactly what I just said. Women think because they pussy good, then they don't have to do shit else. That's a lie and you know it. I want to feel loved and protected too. I want to know that I can depend on my girl if times get hard. What happens if I get caught up in these streets and can't work or go to jail?"

"Stop bringing up stuff like that. You aren't going to no damn jail."

"You don't know that. Do I want to go? Of course not. But we don't know what the future holds. You gotta be prepared for whatever, Ma. I know I've taught you that several times."

"Again, I wasn't working when you met me," she repeated, changing the subject. She hated anytime I reminded her of how dangerous this street life was and how I could end up in jail or dead.

"Aight, Ma. I'm not about to go back and fo-," my statement was interrupted.

"Hang up, baby. Let me put this dick back in your life before I dip," I heard in the background. It was a strong deep manly voice that I heard. The voice sounded familiar to me, but I couldn't place it for shit.

"What the fuck? Who is that?" I questioned Amara.

"That's the TV," she said. I knew she was lying.

"Don't fuckin' play with me, Mara. I'ma fuck you up. Where the fuck you at?"

"I'm at home where you should've been two damn days ago."

"Then who's there with you?"

"It's nobody, baby. You hearing the TV," she lied again.

"Aight. That's how you wanna play? Cool. I got you," I told her and ended the call. She tried calling me back three times and I sent her to the voicemail each time. I wasn't a damn fool.

Tired, I found myself swerving in and out of lanes trying to get home. Amara kept calling me. I'm sure she was trying to see where I was at. So, I decided to play along with the shit. Answering the phone, I didn't bother to say anything.

"I know you didn't just hang up on m…"

Click…

I hung up on her ass again.

Don't get me wrong, I loved Amara. She's actually the first woman I ever loved. Most men would say their mother was the first woman they loved, but I could never.

I grew up in the system. I was bounced from foster home to foster home all because my mother didn't want me. I heard I was the product of rape. She didn't want to have to relive what happened to her every time she looked at me and she could never see herself killing a child by aborting me, so her only option was to give me up. That may have been the best thing for her, but it was real fucked up to me. She'd never understand the things I had to go through because she couldn't love me the way that I needed to be loved. She acted like I was the one who raped her or something. That's neither here nor there. Like I said, Amara was the first woman I ever loved.

Amara and I met when I first started working in the streets. I was a corner boy, just getting into the game. I'd recently graduated from high school and had no plans of going to college. My foster parents told me that since I reached 18, I either had to go to college, get a job, or move out. College was out of the question for me since I was burnt out from my first 13 years in school. Getting a job wasn't something that I was interested in just yet. All I wanted to do was catch up on my sleep and enjoy my last few years as a teenager. They had other plans for me. So, after graduation. I hit the streets.

One day I pulled up at a gas station because the old ass Cutlass that I was driving was running hot. I'd purchased the car about three months after leaving my foster home. There was so much wrong with the car and I couldn't afford to fix it, so I had to deal with whatever problems it had whenever they came up. It wasn't the best car in the world, but it got me from point A to point B.

Parked at a gas pump, I grabbed the empty water jug out my trunk and ran to the bathroom to get some water. I had somewhere to be and my car was slowing me down. The minute I walked back towards my car I saw Amara pull up in a new Honda Accord with a few other girls. She got out the car and went prancing towards the store. Her big onion shaped ass is what did it for me. It bounced like a ball as it swayed when she walked. My dick instantly bricked up at the sight of her. She was gorgeous. At that time, she was the prettiest woman I'd ever laid eyes on. She reminded me of Bernadette Stanis when she played Thelma on Good Times.

Not wanting to be embarrassed any further about what was going on with my car, I waited until she went inside the store before pouring the water in my radiator and cranking the car up. It wasn't crunk a good three minutes before Amara came sashaying back out of the store. That was my cue to approach her. I was wearing a white tee, some jeans, and a dusty pair of Timbs. Remember, I was still at the bottom of the food chain so I couldn't afford much.

"Hello beautiful," I said when I was close up on her. She turned around with a smile that quickly faded as she looked me up and down.

"Eww... What do you want?" she responded, throwing her hands on her hips.

"I'm trying to get to know you, Ma. You looking good as hell out here. Your man know you dressed like that," I asked, referring to the small ass skirt she was wearing that left her booty cheeks freely hanging from the bottom and the tight as halter top that displayed her beautiful perky breasts.

"Yeah, he know; now scat," she spat. The bitch was rude as hell.

"Well, fuck you bitch," I rattled off before walking away from her. That was my very first encounter with her.

My next encounter was when I'd moved up a bit and started making a little more money. I was able to purchase my Camry, get a decent apartment, and dress ten times better. She saw me out at a restaurant with this dude name Majestic. Majestic was the man in these streets. I was trying to get to where he was. He was supposed to train me up, but I kept refusing to work under him. I wanted to do this shit on my own. Allowing him to take me under his wing meant that he'd be trying to get credit for my come up and I didn't want to deal with no shit like that. That's why I refused his offer each time he asked.

"Hey, I remember you," Amara said, reaching out and touching my shoulder. I removed her hands off me and told her to step back. She didn't want me when I didn't have shit so what the fuck made her think I was willing to fuck with her when I made a little come up? I'll tell you what it was. I had to get up and go to the bathroom in the middle of my meal. She followed me in the bathroom and worked magic on my dick with her mouth and pussy. That was it for me. I latched on to her ass three years ago and never let her go.

Ring... Ring... Ring...

My ringing phone removed me from my thoughts. It was Amara calling again. I'd gotten tired of her calling. You would think if someone kept sending you to voicemail, that meant they didn't want to be bothered with your ass. She never got the picture.

"Yeah, just like that baby. Swallow this dick whole," I heard. That bitch tried to play me saying she was watching TV. What the fuck kind of porn was she watching?

"Stupid bitch!" I yelled. I was furious. Amara had me fucked up if she thought I was going to let her get away with cheating on me.

Putting the phone up to my ear, I could hear talking from the other line. It seemed to me that she had butt dialed me. That was fine because I was about to throw her out on her ass.

Swooping into our apartment complex, I parked, hopped out the car and headed for the front door. I didn't even stop to take the key out of the ignition. I already had it made up in my mind that I was leaving because she was cheating. That was something that I wasn't going to tolerate no matter how much I loved and cared about someone.

Reaching the front door, I slowly turned the knob. I was surprised to find it unlocked. That worked out perfectly for me because that meant I could sneak in on her without her knowing it. If she left the door unlocked, I was more than sure that she didn't set the alarm either.

Inside, I didn't waste any time creeping towards the bedroom. I placed my hand on the piece that had been resting on my side. My heart was beating so fast I thought it was going to beat out of my chest. The further I walked towards my room the more moans began to fill my ears. I stopped a few times to pinch myself. I was hoping the shit was a dream, but when I heard the loud smacking sounds, I damn near started letting shots rang throughout the entire room. That nigga was hitting my girl from the back and smacking her ass in the bed that I bought. In the apartment that I paid the mufuckin' bills in. Naw, that shit wasn't going to fly. With my hands on the trigger, I stormed through the house and pushed the bedroom door open so fast, it flew back and hit the wall. If that shit put a

hole in my wall, that was going to be another ass whoopin'
for Amara's ass.

"Bitch, what the fuck are you d-," I interrupted myself
when I noticed what she was doing. The bitch was
standing near the TV with the phone next to it, watching
porn.

"Yeah, you thought there was another nigga in here,
huh? Got yo mufuckin' ass. Now, you see how the fuck I
feel when you don't come home," she muttered. I was
beyond livid. How the fuck she gonna play me like that?
She had porn blasting through the phone to make it seem
like there was another nigga in there with her. The shit
was unreal. As much porn as I've had to watch these past
few months, you would've thought I'd know when I was
listening to real sex or when I was hearing some porn shit.

"This shit not even funny, Amara," I mumbled.

"Why the hell isn't it? You keep leaving me here like this
and see what happens," she warned.

"What the fuck is that supposed to mean? You act like
I'm out here laid up with some hoes or some shit. I'm out
here trying to make money so we can continue to eat."

"You've been doing that shit for years now and you are still at the bottom of the food chain. You need to be like Majestic's ass. Hell, go to that nigga and tell him you want to work for him so you can come up. This nickel and diming shit you doing just ain't working for me."

Amara had a look of distress on her face. Then I noticed her get teary-eyed. Going over towards her, I kissed her on the forehead before apologizing to her.

"Baby, I'm sorry. I know you don't like when I have to leave you like that, but I'm trying to build myself up. There is real competition in these streets. Keep holding me down, baby; I swear our time is coming," I tried my best to assure her. I knew everything I said went in one ear and out the other. I was too tired to want to argue with her. What I wasn't too tired for was to get some head, some pussy, and go my black ass to sleep.

"You gonna make it up to me?"

"Make it up to you how?"

"I saw this purse I really want in the Michael Kors store." If I just told her ass I was out there gathering the money to make sure the bills were paid and we were eating, why the hell would she ask me about a fuckin' purse? Instead of arguing with her, I roughly pushed her against the wall and pressed my lips up against hers.

Amara started pushing me like she wanted me to get off her. She was resisting dick from me and that was something she never did. Even when she was on her cycle, she still wanted to fuck. She claimed she was putting ketchup on my hot dog when I raw dog her during her cycle. It may seem nasty to some people, but that shit was pleasurable as fuck to me. The wetter the better.

"Move back, Zion. I'm not 'bout to do this with you. You were probably fuckin' off on the next bitch and now you wanna come lay up with me. It don't work like that with me," she stated.

"Come on, baby. I'm tired as fuck. A nigga need you more than the air I breathe," I insisted.

"Fine, let me go take a shower first." She continued to try to push me off her, but I wasn't having that.

"Chill out, Ma. You took a shower last night. Come on and let me slide off in it right quick." I felt like I was begging her to give me something that was supposed to be mine in the first damn place. She was on some bullshit and she knew it.

Picking her up, I marched towards the bed and gently laid her down. She was wearing a robe, so it didn't take much for me to undo it. I laid on top of her and peered into her eyes. Something was up with her because she kept turning her face and blinking each time I tried to make eye contact with her.

"What is going on with you?" I asked. Knowing her, there was no way she was going to tell me the truth, so I waited to see what good lie she was going to come up with.

"Nothing is going on. I'm still a little tired from being up all night worrying about you. I needed the shower to help wake me up." I wasn't sure who she was trying to convince, me or herself. Either way, I decided to go with the story she told me.

"You love me?" I don't know what made me ask her that, but something did. There was a naggin' feeling inside of me telling me something wasn't right, but I didn't want to believe that Amara would hurt me when she knew how hard I went for us.

"You know I love you," she replied before placing her hands on the sides of my face and bringing my lips down to meet hers. My dick was bulging through my pants, begging to be set free. I started grinding between her legs to wet her up as we continued to engage in a passionate kiss. After a while, I was ready to taste her.

Slowly, I placed a trail of kisses from her mouth all the way down to her thighs. She slightly began to open her legs for me. I paused for a brief moment because a fish like smell hit me in the face. I knew then why she wanted to go shower first. She must've sweated between the legs. I instantly regretted my decision to not let her go.

"You okay, baby? Why you stop?" she asked me.

"Sorry, I was about to stand up and take my pants off," I lied.

"I'll do that when I get ready to please you. Finish pleasing me first, baby. I've never had a man eat my pussy the way that you do," she said in a low whisper. That caused me to smile because that meant I was doing something right.

One thing I never did was question my ability to please her sexually. The long, deep strokes that I delivered mixed with her loud screams and all the scratches she left on my back let me know that I was a mufuckin' beast with it.

After a while, I commenced to kissing on her thighs. I spread her legs a little further before placing my lip on her clit. I started sucking on it like I was sucking the meat out of crawfish. Her juices tasted so good to me. Feasting on her was something I could've done all day.

"Eat that pussy, baby. Yeah, just like that," she obliged. That's when I slithered my tongue inside her love tunnel. I flicked it up and down and plunged it in and out of her. Amara's moans became louder as I continued pleasuring her. Taking things a step further, I took my index finger and ring finger and inserted them inside of her tunnel while I continued to suck on her clit. Wiggling my fingers around inside of her, I started to feel something.

Stopping, I moved back a little to see what the hell was going on. Moving my fingers a little more, I pinched something inside of her and slowly pulled my fingers from between her legs. My mouth dropped open as the condom I'd just removed from Amara freely dangled between my fingers. She shot up in the bed and just stared at me. What was she supposed to say? There was nothing she could say. She'd fucked up and had just gotten caught. It was only a matter of time before I started fuckin' the entire bedroom up.

Chapter Two:

Amara

I had been walking around on eggshells since Zion and I had a falling out. He was still mad at me, but he's fucked up in the past too. If his ass would just go under Majestic, he would be making so much more money and we wouldn't be arguing so fucking much. Then I wouldn't be out here getting fucked by the next nigga to get what the hell I wanted. Zion always talking about the kids need this or the bills need to be paid. Shit I'm sick of all that. I needed my nails, hair, and lashes done. All of that needed to be ahead of his list just as well as the groceries and bills.

Zion was always fussing about money and bills. I'm the same bitch he met three years and two kids ago.

"Girl what the hell is your problem?" my best friend Rickie asked.

"I'm so sick of this shit with Zion. He wants me to be at home taking care of his kids, cleaning the house, and fucking him on the regular. But he can't buy me what the fuck I want. Then when I say something about it, he'll tell me that I need to get a job to help him out. I know he fuckin' lyin'."

"Mara, Zion is a good dude and he takes good care of the kids and you. So, I'm not understanding what the bitching is for."

Rickie and I went way back, and I hated whenever she was team Zion. She was my best friend and it was no reason why she always had to have his side. I didn't even wanna talk about this shit anymore. I just wanted her to roll up, so I could smoke her shit then put her ass out.

"Bitch roll up, before ZJ and Zaire wake up," I demanded while throwing her the jar of bud that I had just taken from Zion's stash. I planned to smoke her shit and his shit.

My phone started vibrating on the table and caught my attention before I said another word. I already knew who it was since I had been ignoring his calls and shit. I couldn't respond because Zion was already mad with me. I had to let the shit blow over on the home front before I could see him again. Yeah, I cheated on Zion, but so what? Until he starts making more money to take care of me like I deserve, I'ma do me. Since Zion wasn't home, I decided to respond.

Maggie: I see you on good bullshit right now, huh?

Me: I'm sorry you know how shit be.

Maggie: I'm not gone keep doing this shit, Ma.

Me: I know, and I promise you, soon everything will go as planned.

Maggie: I'm gone hold you to that shit. Now make sure you are making your way to see me before this week is out.

Me: Ok, I got you.

Maggie: I mean what I said and if you don't show up, I'll be over there.

Me and my secret lover had been going on for years. Hell, we may have been dealing with each other just as long as Zion and me. I made sure to put him in my phone as *Maggie* so that way Zion would think it's a bitch.

"Mara, you don't hear me calling you?"

"My bad Rickie. What's up?"

"Bitch the blunt is rolled where's the lighter?"

I hurried and snatched the blunt out of her hand then lit it. I was stressed about all of this and I was kind of over it. I loved Zion but he just didn't have all the shit I needed in a man. I wish I could build my own fucking man. Then I could make that nigga everything I needed and wanted. I grew up with two dope head parents, that meant I never had shit. So, at an early age I was making my way around the hood dealing with all the money makers. I still found it hard to believe that I ended up wit Zion's broke ass.

"Damn can I get a pull? What's going on? First, you don't hear me calling you and now you are hogging the damn blunt. What got ya mind all clouded that fast?" Rickie asked, being nosey.

I never told her shit that I did outside of my relationship because I didn't need to hear what I should have been doing like she was my mama instead of my best friend.

Wahhh…Wahhh…Wahhh…

"Mommy, Zi is crying," ZJ said while walking into the living room.

"Boy get ya ass back in that room. All you have to do is put that pacifier in his mouth," I snapped.

Rickie looked at me while shaking her head. I knew she didn't like how I just talked to my son. But the keyword in this was MY son. I could do or say anything I wanted to my damn kids. That was another issue I had with her. She always told me how to raise my damn kids. As long as I fed and kept them laced with the finer things then I was doing good as a mother.

"I think it's time for me to go. Just call me later," Rickie said while taking her last pull of the blunt. After she left, I finished smoking my blunt then I fixed the boys some chicken nuggets and fries.

******

I couldn't chance my lover popping up at my crib and Zion was out like always. So, I ended up taking the kids to his adoptive parents' house. We lived out Pennsauken and they still lived in the city smack dead in the hood. They had a big ass house and their mortgage was cheap as fuck. I kept telling Zion that we could find a big ass house in the hood that way we could have more money. But no, he didn't want his kids in the hood. Hell, he would be mad as hell right now if he knew I had them over here.

"Hey Amara, does my son know you're here?" Ms. Clair asked.

"No, and don't call hm as soon as I leave. You know how he is, but I know you and Mr. Butch haven't seen them in a minute. So, I figured I would bring them over and if you call him that would just make drama. Then I just won't bring them over anymore and don't play with me Ms. Clair," I said. Being honest, they always listened to everything that Zion said like he was they fucking daddy.

"What time will you be back to pick them up? My wife and I will be going to breakfast in the morning, so make sure you be back here at a decent hour. If you don't want me to call my son," Mr. Butch fussed from the living room. He couldn't stand me, and the shit was mutual. He always would tell Zion that he didn't know why he decided to have kids by my rachet ass. I didn't give a fuck though; he was just mad Zion left home and didn't go to college like they stuck up asses wanted. I didn't even respond to his ass. I just kissed my boys then headed out the door. I was going to make sure I made it back at a decent hour so I wouldn't hear their mouths.

Chapter Three:

Majesty

I had just come home from work to see all these cops and an ambulance parked outside of my Nana's home. I didn't park my car all the way; I just jumped out and ran in to see what was going on.

"No, ma'am! You can't go in there." A cop stopped me.

"My name is Majesty Jones and this is my house! Where's my Nana? Where is she?" I cried out, knowing that in my gut something wasn't right.

"Let her in," the other cop said.

"Hello, I'm Detective Lewis. We got a call that there was arguing coming from this home with gun shots shortly after."

"Officer, I went to work this morning and I'm just getting off," I said in a sad tone.

I had no clue what the hell happened here, but I was sure it had something to do with my cousin's Scott crackhead ass. I hated that my Nana wouldn't let him go. He wouldn't stay clean, but she would never put his ass out.

"Are you ok, Ms. Jones?"

"Scott Miller is who you need to be looking for," was all I could say just above a whisper.

"Who's that, Ms. Jones?"

"That's my cousin that she couldn't let go of. The one that needed saving but didn't want saving. Please can I see her?"

The officer let me by and the scene before me broke my heart. She was slumped over in her favorite chair with her purse on the floor and an empty wallet on her lap. I just couldn't contain myself, I let out a gut-wrenching cry. The only person that ever cared about me. The only family that I had in this state was gone. Shit, truth be told, I had no family. Only my big brother Majestic that lived in New Jersey, which was only an hour and forty minutes away. Majestic and I had the same daddy but different crack head mamas. Drug addicted tramps were our low life's choice of women.

The feeling of the officer pulling me into his arms bought me out of my thoughts. I knew I had to let them do their jobs, yet I wasn't ready for my baby to leave this world. But I guess it was God's will.

"You've already identified the body, but we're still going to need your signatures down at the morgue. We also need to talk some more about this Scott character, and I need a picture or description of him; anything to help us get this case closed right now."

I didn't say a word, I just wiped my tears away and then headed back out to my car and hopped in. I would do what I needed to do for the police, but then I needed to go. I needed to find Scott's ass to handle him on my own.

****

After being with the police for hours, I went home, threw on all black, packed a couple of suitcases, and then headed to where I knew Scott would be. I didn't tell the police, but I knew because Nana use to send me to look for him when she hadn't seen him for days. Yeah, he would be dumb for being there, but I was sure by now he was high out of his fucking mind.

I parked my car on the corner of South Gilmor and McHenry Street. This was a hot spot for drug houses here in Baltimore. I jumped out and walked straight up to the door. Of course, I already knew the password. I knocked on the door then said, "Playtime". Who ever thought of this word was an ass. I walked through the house and the shit was just sad. The smell was overbearing, people were slumped over. Others just looked like zombies. I saw all types of shit in here and the shit was sickening. The people in here were so fucking high they were sitting stuck in their own little worlds. I knew when I saw Scott, he was going to be done since I knew he had stolen over a thousand dollars from my Nana. I had just given her that money before I left for work to handle the bills and to get groceries. I knew it wasn't much, but I knew it was what I had until Majestic sent me more.

I had finally made it to Scott's favorite room and just like I suspected, he was slumped over with two raggedy ass bitches with him. I made both the bitches get out and then I shut the door.

"So, you just gone kill the only person who ever gave a fuck about you?"

"Come on JJ, now you know I didn't do that shit." He had the nerve to lie while his eyes rolled back in his head.

"Nigga don't call me JJ!" I snapped while hitting him across the face with the butt of my gun.

Scott then looked at me with a bloody mouth and then he just started laughing at me. The shit had me angry as hell, so I hit him again with the gun.

"All the old bitch had to do was give me the money. It's like ever since you moved in, she didn't fuck with me anymore. You got all of her attention. I wish your crack head ass mama didn't leave you on our doorstep. You killed Nana, not me. If she didn't care so much about what you thought and just gave me what I asked for she would still be here."

Hearing him say that pissed me the fuck off even more. I placed my finger on the trigger and blew his fucking brains out. I then wiped the gun off and placed it in his hands like he killed himself. I walked out of the door never turning back. I jumped in my car and sat there for a while to gather my thoughts. I would come back in a couple of days to handle my Nana's arrangements. All she wanted was to be cremated, so I would call the funeral home and have all of that taken care of while I was in Jersey. I had no one left, but my brother and I guess it was time for me to pay him a visit. He acted like he didn't care for me, but he made sure I was always good. I think he hated the fact that our daddy cheated on his mama with my mama. Hell, we both should hate our parents and love each other because of what we went through. But it was different for us and I wasn't going to make no one love me. Once I got my thoughts together, I peeled off making my way to my brother's house.

Exactly an hour and forty-five minutes later, I was pulling up to my brother's house. He still had heavy security posted up and all I could do was shake my head. Our parents were the biggest crack heads ever and here his ass go being a fucking king pin. The shit was crazy, that was what he chose to do, and the money kept me straight so who was I to judge? I just made sure I didn't need to depend on him and his money which is why I always kept a job. After pulling into the gate I had to tell the guard who I was. He made a call and then let me right in. I had to drive down this long path until I made my way to the big ass house that sat on the hill. I saw two people standing on the porch, so I hurried and jumped out. My brother was standing on the porch talking to this chick. It was late as hell so I knew she must be a jump off because it was no way I was going to let some nigga dick me down then I had to take the walk of shame.

I don't know what the fuck came over me, but the minute I hit the top step the tears started to run down my face, and I ran right into my brother's arms.

"Ssssshhhhhh…JJ what the fuck is going on?" he asked while hugging me back.

"She's dead Majestic! My Nana is dead," I managed to get out before crying uncontrollably.

"MAJESTIC! Who the fuck is this?" the chick had the nerve to say while sucking her teeth.

I looked at her with so much anger before speaking. "Bitch, don't worry about who the fuck I am, go on ahead home. Like you were headed before I pulled up. Take ya walk of shame quietly and don't worry about who the fuck I am."

Majestic chuckled, "Go in the house right quick JJ and let me talk to her."

"So, that's what we do now. We let ya bitches disrespect me Majestic?" I heard the bitch say while I walked in the house. I knew Majestic didn't care for me. But I knew he would never let anyone disrespect me or hurt me. The way he just hugged me though made me feel like he may have liked me just a little bit.

Chapter Four:

Majestic

"What I tell you about being jealous? I told you that you the only bitch I'm fuckin' with," I told ol' girl. We'd been fuckin' around for a minute and it was sad to say, but I somewhat loved her mean ass.

"I'm sorry, but you know how I get over you."

"Well you need to pipe down with all of that. I can barely handle your ass. What the fuck I look like trying to control another bitch? Besides, if I did, you know damn well that I wouldn't let them hoes know where I lived," I reminded her.

Amara was everything to me. When I met her, it was only supposed to be a one-night stand, but one dip in her ocean and a nigga was hooked. The fact that I knew I could always depend on her also played a major role in me stickin' with her ass. However, I knew she had a nigga. That was the only thing fuckin' with me.

See, when I met Amara, I had a bitch that I stayed with on a regular. She wanted me to give her up, but I couldn't because the girl kept saying she was pregnant. One thing about me, I would never turn my back on my own seeds.

My parents may have not been able to save me from these streets, but they did instill the value of family in me. Not by choice though. They weren't much of parents, but they taught me the type of parent that I wanted to be. Hence me being big on family. There was no way I was going to let somebody that was carrying my child be out on the street.

Phaedra and I had been fucking around, off and on, for about a year. When I'd grown tired of her ass and told her I was ready to walk away, that's when she hit me with the shit that she was pregnant. I had the bitch piss on a stick in front of me and sure as shit, she was pregnant. I allowed her to move in with me and everything. Things started off okay but then she started to be too clingy. I hated that shit. Amara was like that at times, but I'd quickly remind her that being clingy would get you put out of my life fast, quick, and in a mufuckin' hurry.

One day Phaedra had a doctor's appointment and she knew I wanted to go with her. She told me she would call and let me know the time of the appointment. I made sure I didn't have shit to do because we were supposed to get one of those pictures of the baby and shit. A nigga was amped up about that shit. I wanted to see my lil' niglet, even if I couldn't really make out what the fuck I was looking at. As the day progressed, I waited and waited for her call, but it never came. Around 3:00 that evening, I called her ass to see what the fuck was up. The bitch had the nerve to tell me that they called her and had her come in earlier. She said she didn't want to bother me because she knew I'd be busy. That shit fucked with me. We got into it and I spazzed out on her ass. I told her to stay the fuck away from me and hung up on her. I got together with some of my boys and we hit the clubs. That's when I laid eyes on Amara.

Amara had always been beautiful to me. She had on these lil' short ass black shorts that looked like boy shorts with some pink ass tube top and some pink wedges. She was dressed ratchet as hell, but I overlooked that. It was something about her almond shaped eyes that I couldn't get enough off. I had to have her. I shot my shot and a nigga been fuckin' her ever since. I told her from the jump about my situation with Phaedra. She wasn't mad because she had a situation of her own going on. That was how we were able to keep fuckin' around without the people we were serious with finding out about us. We had an understanding and as long as neither of us breached what we agreed upon, we were cool.

Long story short, I later found out that Phaedra had ordered that pregnancy test offline that would give a false positive. The reason her bitch ass didn't want me going to the doctor was because she didn't want me knowing the truth. The bitch even had the nerve to buy one of those pregnant pillow shits and walked around with it on. You'd thought I'd catch that, right? Naw, because when she claimed she was getting bigger, we stopped fuckin' or when we did, she'd keep her shirt on. I was getting the pussy so that shit never dawned on me that she was on some bullshit. The moment I realized what she was on, I had Amara beat the breaks off her ass because I didn't hit women. The fact that Amara did it let me know she was goin' to ride with me no matter what.

Now that I was single, I stayed focused on my money and my girl. I wanted her to come home to daddy, but she keeps reminding me that she had her own situation going on with her nigga and her two kids. I couldn't be mad because I knew what it was from jump. Not to mention, I would never destroy a child's family. That wasn't the type of nigga that I was. Besides, I knew it was only a matter of time before Amara came to be with me. She wanted the finer things in life. The things that only I could give her. I was just counting the days down until we were together for good.

"Baby, are you listening to me? I got to go pick the kids up and make it home before Zion does," she whined. I knew her spoiled ass didn't want to leave me. Especially, not after the dick I just dumped off in her. But her kids came first, so I understood that.

"Aight, go handle your business. Let me go and see what's going on with my sister," I announced.

"Your sister? You never told me you had a sister," she replied. Her eyes seemed to light up immediately.

"Trust me, I wish I didn't. Ain't shit I can do about it though," I muttered.

"Well, let me meet her being that I'm your girl and all. I think it's about time that I started to meet your family," she commented.

"Aight. That's cool. Then we going to leave here and you're going to take me to meet your family, right?" Amara's eyes got big as hell. She didn't have to say shit to me because I already knew what it was. "Exactly. Don't be trying to make me do shit that you obviously not ready for. I'll get at you later," I told her and then walked inside without giving her a chance to say anything in return. There was really nothing left for her ass to say anyways.

"Sis?" I called out as soon as I was inside the crib.

"I'm in here," she responded. The sadness was all in her tone. I hated the fact that she existed because of the way she got here, but I couldn't turn my back on her because it wasn't her fault that our father wasn't shit.

"Now, what's going on?" I stood in the doorway and asked. I wasn't a sentimental person, so I didn't really know how to comfort her.

"When I got home from work and went to Nana's house, there were cops everywhere. I could already think in my head what could've happened, but I was in denial. I didn't want the shit to be true. You had to have seen her, Maj. He killed her like she wasn't shit. Scott killed her over money. It's all my fault. If I didn't give her that money, he wouldn't have had a reason to go after her. If I would've missed work and been there the-"

"Then he probably would've killed your ass too," I interrupted her. "I'm not trying to come off as mean but cut the bullshit. There wasn't shit you could've done. If you were there, then you probably wouldn't be here right now because he would've gotten your ass too. You and I grew up pretty much the same way. With mothers who chose crack over us. You and I both know that when they are fiending for the shit, there ain't a damn thing anybody can do about it and they are willing to do whatever they have to do to get it," I concluded.

"It's just not fair. She died alone and she didn't deserve that," she cried.

"Roseeeeeee," I called out. Rose was my maid and had worked for me for years. I wasn't the type of person to comfort anyone, but Rose had kids. I knew she'd know what to do.

"Yes sir?" She rushed inside the room.

"Take care of my sis, I got some shit to handle," I ordered.

"I already handled it," Majesty announced.

"You what? You handled it?" I questioned with a voice full of shock. Instead of answering, she nodded her head up and down. "Damn... Rose step out for a second."

With Rose out of the room, I walked closer to Majesty and sat down next to her. "Are you sure you handled it?"

"Yes."

"With?"

"CeCe." CeCe was the name she gave to the purple Taurus I'd purchased for her last year.

"Where is CeCe?"

"She's with Lexus." Lexus was the type of car that she drove.

Majesty wasn't in the streets, but she knew what I did. She hated it, but she had no choice but to respect it because the money I earned helped her out a lot. She knew that it was dangerous, and that it was a must that we talked in code. We pretty much had a code word for everything. When you use names, it's easier and makes it harder for others to figure out. The whole time we were talking about objects, they'd be thinking we were talking about people and be looking for people that didn't exist.

Yeah, we were smart like that. Truth be told, it was Majesty's idea to do it that way.

"I'll go take care of Lexus and CeCe. Don't worry, I'll make sure you get everything that belongs to you out of it. Let Rose take you to a room and help you get comfortable. We can talk a little more about this after you've eaten and got some sleep. Cool?" She nodded her head.

Once I'd gotten Rose to help her get situated, I called my crew. I had them strip down Majesty's car and get rid of it. Money wasn't a problem, so I'd just upgrade her ass tomorrow. I was tired and ready to lay it down for the night. When I got to my room and checked my phone, there were several texts from Amara going off because she didn't like the way I handled her before she left. I chose not to respond to either of them. After a while, a text came through telling me that she had made it home and that she loved me. I hit her ass with the thumbs up emoji and turned my phone off. Already knowing it was going to be a long day tomorrow, I took a quick shower and crawled in the bed. The money I got was everything but the life I lived was tiresome. Many nights I questioned if it was really worth it.

Chapter Five:

Zion

Amara had me fucked up. As soon as she dropped the kids off at my adoptive parent's house, they called and told me. They even told me how she threatened to never bring the kids around them again if they told me. I didn't have a problem with them seeing the kids, I just didn't like the neighborhood they lived in. I told them that once I started making more money, I was going to take them away from the hood and I meant that shit.

Pacing the breezeway of the complex, I couldn't wrap my mind on what the fuck the bitch was thinking. She knew how I felt about my kids and for her to put them in a dangerous situation had me beyond heated. She was probably out on the next nigga's dick thinking I wasn't gonna say shit, but she was dead ass wrong. I should've left her ass the night I found that fuckin' condom in her, but all I could think about were my kids. She didn't have money and I'm sure no place else to go. I was always in the streets, so there was no way I could stay with the kids and make money at the same time. I had no choice but to keep her bitch ass around. Then she reminded me of the fact that I cheated on her when we first got together. That was another reason I stuck around. If our kids didn't exist, I would've been dipped on her dog ass. Yeah, I said dog ass because Amara's ass was worse than a nigga.

Bright lights turning into the parking lot removed me from my thoughts. As soon as I saw that it was Amara's ass, I charged straight towards the car. I went around to the driver's side and snatched Amara's ass out the car.

"What the fuck are you doing?" she had the nerve to ask me.

"Don't ask me a mufuckin' thing. Where the hell your hoe ass been with my kids?" I already knew the answer to that, but I wanted to see if she was going to lie.

"I had to go take care of something."

"Bitch, you don't see what time it is?" I chided. "The only thing open at this time of night is a bitch's legs. Let me guess, I'm going to find another condom inside of you."

"Let that shit go, Zion. I told you I fucked up that one time. I'm not going to cheat on you ever again. I love you, baby." The way she said it caused my body to shudder. She was full of shit and we both knew it.

"Move the fuck out of my way. I'm not doing this shit with you, Amara," I fussed.

Letting her go, I went around to the other side of the car to retrieve my kids and the diaper bag. I took them inside the apartment and immediately to their room. They were both sleep, but I couldn't let them go to bed without taking a bath. So, one at a time, I took them inside the bathroom and cleaned them from head to toe before putting them on some clean clothes and tucking them into their beds.

When I stepped inside the bedroom I shared with Amara, I couldn't even look at her ass. She was laid on the bed with her legs gapped open. She'd taken her panties off and pulled her dress up to almost around her neck, pleasing herself with her vibrator.

"Come touch me, baby," she instructed. I acted like her ass wasn't there. I was long overdue for some pussy, but I didn't want hers. That shit was used and abused. She could keep giving it to the next nigga for all I cared. "Baby, you don't hear me talking to you?"

"I hear everything you're saying, but I'm not fuckin' with you like that," I explained.

"What the hell is that supposed to mean? You said you forgave me."

"No, I never said I forgave shit. I said I wasn't going to leave your dusty ass because of my kids. Just because I'm here with you doesn't mean that I'm going to be fuckin' you."

"I know you Zion. You love pussy too much to go without it. If you're not getting it from me then you're getting it from somewhere else. You cheating on me again?" She sat up in the bed and stared me down.

"I don't have time for this shit. There are more things in this world than your dried-up ass pussy. I'm not fuckin' with you like that anymore and I mean that shit," I fumed and continued on with what I was doing. I'd had enough of Amara's ass for the night. I opted to sleep on the couch that was in the room with the kids. I'd rather be in there than to spend another minute laid up in the same bed with Amara's ass. That's how pissed off I was at her. She was out hoeing and whether she wanted to admit it or not, I knew the damn truth.

"Don't do this, Zion. I told you I was sorry. I said it wouldn't happen again and I meant that. Let's work this out," she pleaded with me.

"I can't even take you serious," I told her.

"Why? I'm being honest with you," she whined.

"You may be honest with me but that nut stain on your dress is being honest with me too and telling me how big of a hoe your ass really is," I retorted, pointing to the dried-up white streak on her dress. Whomever she was with must've really wanted her ass because they constantly left me signs of their rendezvous, so I'd know when her ass was lying. Sucked for her because it was only a matter of time before I stopped fuckin' with her ass altogether.

"Nut stain? Where?" she asked, jumping up and pulling her dress off to inspect it. I shook my head, grabbed my pillow and the comforter off the bed and left out the room. There wasn't shit else left for us to talk about.

*****

I didn't get the best sleep. The couch in the kid's room was leather and uncomfortable as hell. I contemplated sleeping on the fuckin' floor but I knew that would've been worse. The next morning, I got up and got them dressed before fixing them breakfast.

"Where's my plate?" Amara had the nerve to come into the kitchen and ask. Being petty, I walked over to one of the cabinets and pulled a plate out. I handed it to her and kept walking. "Seriously? How long are you going to be acting this way with me?"

"Until I no longer have to deal with your ass," I honestly spoke. "Now, I have some business to take care of. Watch my babies. If something happens to them, I'm going to fuck you up," I warned her.

"You know I would never let anything happen to them. Stop being this way with me."

"Stop being a hoe," I replied. Shrugging my shoulders, I kissed my kids and left out the kitchen. I was already dressed so I grabbed my keys, wallet, and phone and left the house.

Amara and I had always talked about me working with this nigga named Majestic. He was the man in these streets. I'd avoided working with him for several reasons, but the main reason was that whenever someone who worked for him got caught up, they'd mysteriously end up dead. I knew he had something to do with it because if the person was dead, they wouldn't be able to snitch on his ass. I didn't want to put my life on the line like that. However, since Amara decided she wanted to be a little hoe, it was high time for me to start making major moves. I needed to secure a bag so that I'd be able to afford childcare or even to move my adoptive parents to another neighborhood and allow them to watch the kids for me. No matter what choice I went with, I knew I was going to need money to make it happen and Majestic was the person to help me get that money.

Majestic had me meeting him at a park. I'm not sure why we couldn't just chop it up at one of his other spots, but it was all good. I guess he had to be sure he could trust me. When I pulled up, he was already there with about six other niggas. They were some big ass burly, King Kong lookin' muthafuckas. I grabbed my piece and stuck it in my back in case I got out there and he was on some bullshit. I learned enough to know I couldn't go into shit unprotected.

Before I could step out the car, my door flew open. "You might as well slide that bitch back up under the seat because you can't meet the boss man like that," a deep voice told me. I looked up and it was one of the niggas I'd seen standing over there with Majestic. For the life of me, I couldn't understand how his big ass made it over to my car without me seeing him.

Placing the gun under the seat as I was directed, I got out of the car and allowed dude to pat me down before marching towards Majestic.

"Chill out, lil' nigga. Don't come this way like you got something you need to get off your chest," Majestic stated to me.

"What? That's how I walk," I lied. I was really annoyed at the way he was handling me.

"Yeah, and I'm Santa Clause," he replied. "Now, why you hit me up?" he asked, pulling on the blunt he was lighting when I was walking towards him.

"I need to make some money so I can give my kids the life I never had. I tried working for myself but the shit ain't working out for me. I have a nice little clientele and all, but I need to be bringing in the big bucks, ya feel me?" I explained.

"Why should I trust you? I don't know you." My face squinched up. That nigga had been knowing me for years. I knew his ass was fuckin' with me but I really didn't feel like playing with his ass.

"Come on, Majestic. We've been knowing each other for years. I really need you to help a nigga out. I have two kids depending on me and I can't keep doing this corner boy shit," I admitted.

"I'll tell you what, I'm willing to give you a trial run. If you can't handle yourself accordingly and make the money I think you should be making, it's a wrap and I don't want you to ever approach me again about working with me. You understand?"

"Damn, you cold blooded," I told him. It really aggravated me the way he was acting when he had been practically begging me to work for his ass for a while now. If he thought I was going to beg his ass then he had the game fucked up.

"That's how I got to be, or niggas will stay trying to get over on me. I don't mind helping people out that I know that's trying but I also have to look out for me. I'm running a business and have been for years. I'm not trying to bring nobody on that can take me or my business down."

"I gotcha. I promise you won't be disappointed," I told him.

One of his men handed me a phone and he said he would call me later with what he wanted me to do. That was another reason I didn't want to work for Majestic. He was too fuckin' bossy. I didn't need a nigga standing over me and watching my every move. For all that, he might as well hold my dick while I go to the bathroom and tell me how the fuck to piss. The shit was crazy. I told myself that I was only going to be working with him until I had enough money to move my folks, get rid of Amara's ass, and start legit businesses so I could leave the street shit alone. I said it and that was exactly what was about to happen.

Chapter Six:

Majesty

It had been exactly a week since my Nana's services, and I was still trying to get my life in order. I was having a hard time adjusting, but Rose and Majestic had been a big help. Now it was time for me to go out and find a job. I knew my brother had money, but like I said before, I didn't like to depend on him. I also was going to head over to the Art Institute of Philadelphia. I figured it was time for me to put my ability to draw to use. I see a lot of people love to purchase African American art online. Majestic said he could find an art gallery to sell my drawings in, but I wanted to do this the right way. So, I would rather start from the bottom and work my way up.

"Good morning sweetheart!" Rose said as I walked into the dining room.

"Good morning Rose!" I said while sitting at the table for breakfast.

One thing about my brother was he wanted us to always sit to have breakfast and dinner together. No matter what's going on in life he felt like they were the most important meals of the day and they didn't need to be missed unless it was an emergency.

"Mr. Majestic said he will be joining you shortly," Rose said while beginning to place different dishes of food on the table. This lady made different types of breakfast dishes everyday like it was a lot of us eating. The sound of two voices bought me out of my daze. I looked up and Majestic and his right hand man Kade were both entering the dining room.

Kade was fine but he just wasn't my type. I refused to deal with a nigga that was just like my brother. Yeah, I knew being in the streets was a way to eat, but it didn't have to be the end result of life. I felt like all the money they got in the game should be used as a stepping stool to get out one day.

"What's up ladies?" Kade asked while sitting at the table. Rose didn't say anything which lead me to believe she didn't like his ass. I smirked while shaking my head before I said anything.

"Hey Kade! Good morning Bro," I spoke to the both of them.

"How did you sleep JJ?" Majestic asked.

"Ok, still having nightmares but I'll be ok."

"You'll be good soon sis. What's your plans today?"

"I'm going job hunting and to the Art Institute to apply."

"Let me know the cost of school when you get it all figured out and I'll pay for it all."

I didn't want him to pay for it, but I knew it would help me out a lot, so I didn't refuse.

"Ok, I'll give you the paperwork when I come back in later today."

There was a knock at the door and Rose went to get it. In came Zion, he was a new face that I all a sudden started seeing around here a couple of days ago. Now he was a fine brother too, but he didn't give me the same vibe as Kade. I knew he must have been new to the crew, but what shocked me was Majestic allowed him in his home and he was just now meeting him. That was very shocking to me.

"Good morning everyone!" Zion said while walking in the dining room.

"Hello Zion!" I said, not realizing how big the smile was on my face.

"Hello Mr. Zion! Will you be joining us for breakfast too?" Rose asked.

"Yes, I don't mind joining. I didn't get a chance to eat this morning since I had to get the kids ready before I headed out," Zion said while sitting down.

"Rose always cooks plenty so you're welcome whenever bro," Majestic assured Zion.

After Rose placed another plate on the table, we all dug in. No words were really spoken; we all just ate in silence until Kade decided to ask me something.

"So, JJ when can I see them drawings you be doing?" Kade asked.

"First of all, don't call me JJ. Only people who are close to me call me that. You can call me Majesty."

"Damn, you always so mean to a nigga."

"I'm, not being mean Kade. I'm just not interested, and you be trying way too hard," I said while grabbing a piece of bacon off my plate and getting up from the table.

"You good sis?" Majestic asked.

"Yes, I'm good. I have things to do so it's time to get my day started. Once I get back, I'll give you the information from the school, so you can make the payments. I love you and be safe today," I said while hurrying out the house, but not before I looked at Zion and smiled. I could feel Kade burning a hole in my damn back, but I didn't give a damn; I wasn't interested in him. He just didn't seem to get the picture.

Once I finally made it out of the door, I looked at my new car that Majestic bought in 'aww'. His ass was always extra. I just needed a simple ass car, but he would go out and get me a custom hot pink 2019 Mustang GT. He had to know somebody because ain't no way he got this car painted and bought over here in four days. Either that or he spent a grip getting it. I loved how Majestic took care of me, but I wasn't like that. I didn't need all the hottest shit. After getting myself situated and turning my music up I peeled off and made my way to my first destination. I guess being down here with my brother won't be too bad after all.

Chapter Seven:

Majestic

It was nice having Majesty around the house. Not because I enjoyed a woman being there, but because we weren't exactly close growing up. At least now, we could make up for all the time we missed out on together. The only problem with her always being around was me having to defend my relationship with her to Amara. It seemed like every time something was going right with Amara, she found a reason to bring Majesty up and why she felt Majesty shouldn't be in the house with me. It had gotten old and I decided it was time for me to put my foot down.

"Hey baby," Amara came prancing into the house. I was sitting on the couch tuned in to the news because I liked to keep up with what's going on in the world.

"Sup?" I said, never taking my eyes off the TV. As bad as I wanted to do more to acknowledge her, I couldn't; she needed to learn that she couldn't keep throwing her little tantrums and thinking the shit was going to fly.

"Sup? Fuq you mean by sup?" She looked around the room before training her eyes on me.

"Sup?" I asked again, this time locking eyes with her.

"Don't play with me, Jestic. I'm not one of your lil' side bitches. I'm your woman and you're going to respect me as such," she rattled off, throwing her hands on her hips.

"Are you my woman?" I questioned.

"What is that supposed to mean?"

"It means that you have been acting childish as fuck since my sister came into the picture. I've been dealing with a lot of bullshit from you, but it's time I draw the line." I could tell she knew where I was going with things because she instantly began pouting and came stomping towards me.

"But babyyyyyy..." she whined.

"But baby my ass. You heard what I said. I don't understand how you could get jealous of my sister. I don't do that ancestor shit!" I announced.

"That what?" she curiously questioned.

"That ancestor shit," I repeated.

"What the hell is that?"

"You know that's the shit where them folks be sleeping with their cousins, mothers, fathers, sisters, brothers, and shit. I don't get down like that." Out of nowhere, Amara fell out laughing. My left eyebrow raised as if I were the Rock as I watched and waited to find out what was so damn funny.

"Why you laughing, Ma?"

"I'm laughing because your ass is crazy. Don't ever go out in public and say that shit," she replied.

"Say what shit?" I quizzed, still wondering what was so funny.

"Baby, you are trying to say incest. You don't do incest." When she told me what I was supposed to have said and what I did say, I couldn't help but laugh myself. I sounded dumb as fuck. I was glad I said it to her and not anybody else. They would've thought a nigga never graduated high school.

"Damn, my bad, baby. You knew what the fuck I meant," I stated before laughing a few more times and then straightening my face up.

"I knew what you meant, and I understand what you're saying. Maybe a little more time with her would make things a little better. What you think?" she suggested.

"What I think about what?" I knew what she was saying, but I thought she was out of her mind. She didn't like my sister, and everyone could see that. Shit, even Ray Charles wouldn't be blind to the shit. That was more than enough reason for me to tell her to try that shit again. There was no way I was going to allow her to get close to my sister, say the wrong shit, and they really be beefing. Amara had a mouth on her, but Majesty had hands on her. Allow the beauty to full you and fuck around and end up swallowing your teeth.

"Stop playing with me, Jestic. I want to spend some girl time with your sister. At some point she's going to be my sister-in-law so now is as good of a time as any for us to hang out and start to get to know each other better. I promise you will see a change in the way we interact with each other," she tried reasoning with me. Just as I was about to respond to her, Majesty came walking in the house. She looked as if she'd lost her best friend. I knew it was because she'd just buried her grandmother. I'd never been in her shoes so there was really nothing I could say to make her feel better, so I didn't even try. I did, however, let her know constantly that I was always going to be around if she needed me.

"You good, sis?" I asked her. She came inside the living room and slumped down on the couch.

"I guess I have no choice but to be. If you would've told me a year ago today that I'd have to bury my best friend, I'd never believe it. I can't believe crack was the cause of her death," she ranted.

"It wasn't the crack; it was the dummy with the crack. We have to do better with the things we say are causing other problems in our lives," Amara chimed in. If you could've seen the look on Majesty's face, you would've thrown your church finger up and tiptoed out of this book.

"Majestic, I can understand you trying to be comforting, but I don't do fake. Tell your vulture to take that bullshit to someone else," she snapped. I knew it was coming. I just didn't know when.

"Excuse me," Amara spoke. She stood straight up and stared Majesty down. Majesty stood from where she was once slumped on the couch and walked up on Amara. There was really nothing I could say because Amara had been asking for it. We knew that what she said to Majesty was to throw shade, not to be sincere. Now, she was about to eat her words.

"You heard exactly what I said. Everything about your ass is plastic from your eyelashes down to the damn nails on your toes. I don't need you trying to come to me acting as if you're concerned when we both know that you've had a problem with me being here from day one." Amara looked over at me like she was waiting for me to say something. I threw my hands up as if I were being defeated. I didn't have a dog in that fight. Amara had been wrong for a while and now she was going to have to deal with the consequences.

"You just gonna sit there and let her talk to me like that?" she asked me after Majesty had gone off on her ass.

"Let me? Baby, I'm not suckin' or ridin' his dick. He can't let me do anything. Furthermore, you wouldn't be getting this heat if you would've kept your fuckin' mouth shut. You hate that you have to compete with me to get time with my brother. MY BROTHER! Blood over everything," Majesty yelled before leaving out the room. I couldn't contain my laughter. I grabbed ahold of my side and was leaned over the couch. That was how bad I was laughing. Amara didn't find anything to be funny. Shit, if I were her, I wouldn't see the shit as being funny either.

Amara very quickly saw that I wasn't about to say anything about her little altercation with Majesty. She knew just as well as I did that, she was wrong for the comment that she made. We sat in the living room in complete silence.

"I'm trying. I really am," Amara finally spoke.

"Let it go. You messed up your chances of having a relationship with her the first day that you met her. She's going through a lot right now. At this point, you need to give her time to decide if she's willing to build a relationship with you or not."

Majesty and Amara meant the world to me and it would make my life ten times easier if they could get along. I can't make them do it, so to keep my peace, I made up in my mind that I was going to have to keep them apart for now. That meant having to split my time between the two of them which was going to be a problem for me. Neither of them thought about that when they decided they were going to beef with each other.

"Try Jesus, not me; 'cause I throw hands. Try Jesus, please don't try me. Because I fight." Majesty came walking back through the living room singing *Try Jesus* by

Tobe Nwigwe. When she said that she wasn't fuckin' with Amara, she meant that shit and had no problem making that known to her.

Chapter Eight:

Zion

Amara left the house earlier today and I hadn't heard from her. You'd think she'd at least have the decency to call and check on the kids. She claimed she loved me and wanted things to work between us, but she did everything but showed me how she felt. When I wasn't working the streets, I had my kids. She complained no matter when I had them. She could've watched them for five minutes and that was a problem. I'd never met a woman in my life that was so sorry for being a mother.

We'd just left the park. I needed to run to Wal-Mart to get something to cook and plus I promised I'd get them a new toy. It was really time to get them some more clothes and shoes, but I was going to wait a while so I could save up a little more money. I wanted them to be able to get the clothes and things that they wanted and not be stuck with just getting the things I could afford.

"Excuse me, but I think he just threw his pacifier," a woman spoke, tapping me on the shoulder. When I turned to look at the woman, I was instantly in shock when I saw it was Majesty. I swear she was sexy as hell.

"I'm sorry, what did you say?" I asked. I heard her loud and clear the first time, but I wanted to talk to her a little longer.

"I was just letting you know that your baby dropped his pacifier," she repeated. She bent down and picked the pacifier up off the floor. "Here..." She was about to hand it to me but stopped. I intently watched as she pulled some napkins out of her purse along with a bottled water. She sat the pacifier in the napkins and poured some water over it before washing it off with the napkin and handing it back to Zi.

"Move..." ZJ stated to her. She thought it was funny, but I looked at him like he'd lost his mind. Amara had taught him that shit. As soon as he could talk and comprehend things, she told him that whenever a woman got next to me, he needed to tell them to move.

"I'm sorry, lil' man. I just wanted to keep your brother from crying. You don't want him crying, do you?" Majesty said to ZJ. ZJ just shook his head. "Me either. He's too cute to cry and so are you. What's your name, handsome?" she asked him. The way she was finessing his little ass was hilarious. There he was thinking he was looking out for his nothing ass mama and Majesty quickly made him forget about the shit. I was laughing on the inside.

"Zion Jr.," he said, smiling.

"I'll take it you're Zion Sr." She looked up at me and winked.

"I'm whomever you want me to be," I cracked.

"Cute. I can see where they get it from," she replied. For a minute, I thought a nigga was blushing.

"You're not so bad yourself," I finally replied, licking my lips.

"Thank you." She turned her head just as she said it, so I knew for sure she was blushing.

"Your name is Majesty, right?" I asked.

"Yes," she said when she was able to stop laughing. "You have some really beautiful kids," she told me. I couldn't help but to smile at her like I always had from the first time I met her. I had been checking her out from the first time we were introduced at Majestic's house. I knew I couldn't say anything because of where we were and not wanting to hear shit from Majestic. Now that we were alone, it was the perfect time for me to make my move.

"Thank you."

"My gufrien," ZJ said and pushed me back a little. Me and Majesty fell out laughing.

"My bad, playa. Can't I get the name of my future daughter-in-law?" I asked playing.

For some reason, we stood there in silence. There was evident chemistry between us, but neither of us moved on it. Hell, it had been a while since I hit on a woman. Not because I didn't want to, but because they always hit on me. Not to mention, I called myself being faithful to Amara's raggedy ass. That shit was gone out the window though. Since she wanted to be a hoe, she was going to do that on someone else's time. My two boys were the only reason her stankin' ass had a place to lay her head. If it wasn't for them, she'd probably be laid up somewhere stankin'. Would I have killed her? Nope. That didn't mean shit. With the type of business that I dabbled in, it wouldn't take more than a rock for me to get her ass sent to hell.

"Well, it was nice seeing you," Majesty said, removing me from my thoughts.

My eyes traveled from her feet all the way up to the top of her head. I had to get one more look at her before she walked away. She couldn't have been more than 5' 6. She was short, but I loved that shit. The shorter, the funner. Her nude colored skin complexion and honey brown eyes did something to me. They were slanted like cat-eyes and matched her high cheek bones and beautifully full lips. It didn't take me long to notice the beauty mark that sat above the right side of her lip or the deep dimple that was etched in her right cheek. She also had a small mole under her left eye. That brought her eyes out more to me. I was in love already. Her body was banging to say the least. She was tone and stacked at the same time. Her breast and ass weren't too big and they sure as hell weren't too small. She had a body like Angela Bassett for sure. She was a true Goddess.

"Do you mind if I get your number?" I finally worked up the courage to ask.

"I'm not sure their mother would be happy about that." She pointed to the boys.

"Their mother has no say in what I do with my life. Now, if you're trying to say that you don't want to talk to me because I have children, then say that. These are the only two that I have, and they are by the same woman. I was true to her which is more than I can say about her. I can't erase the fact that I have children or who I had them by, and I'm not trying to. They are my world, and nobody will ever change that." Before I knew it, I was heated. I'm not sure what she was trying to insinuate, but it seemed to me that she had a problem with me having children. That wasn't going to fly with me. I didn't give a damn how fine she was. My boys were everything to me and whomever I ended up with needed to understand that we were a packaged deal.

"Listen, that was not what I was saying. I was actually trying to see if you were still with her. Maybe it came out wrong, but I would never have a problem with you having children. I think they are adorable and thought you looked damn good. But at the same time, you should've asked what I meant instead of trying to check me. I may be cute but don't let this cute face fool you, I throw hands." The tension in my body eased after listening to her explain.

That left me no choice but to apologize to her for the way I came off.

"I'm sorry, I didn't mean it. You run into so many people that judge others for having kids and I think they are the biggest blessing on earth."

"I couldn't agree with you more. At the same time, that doesn't mean you have to be snappy when someone asks about them or their mother. I'm not sure what you've been through and at this point, I'm not sure I care to know. Have a good day," she said and tried to walk around me. I grabbed her by her elbow and pulled her back into me.

Majesty's sweet Japanese Cherry Blossom scent was intoxicating. I loved a woman that only used light body sprays and didn't bathe themselves in perfume. The small amount of mascara she applied to give her lashes a fuller look mixed with the generous amount of lip gloss she wore intrigued me more. That let me know that she wasn't materialistic and believed in natural beauty. I could appreciate that.

"I'm not trying to cause a scene, but I will yell if you don't let me go."

"The way your body is reacting to me lets me know that you really don't want me to let you go. You like me just as much as I like you. Stop playing and give me your number so we can explore and see where things can go," I commented.

"I don't know what you think you feel, but my body isn't reacting in no way at all to you. Now, let me go." The more she fought me, the more turned on I became. I glanced down and saw ZJ looking at me. I didn't want him to think I was hurting her. The only thing I could think to do to get her to stop struggling with me was to begin kissing her neck.

The minute my lips touched her neck, it was almost as if she were melting in my arms. She stopped struggling and soft moans began to escape her mouth.

"Don't." (Kiss) "Keep." (Kiss) "Fighting." (Kiss) "Me." (Kiss) Between each word, I placed a kiss on her neck. When I felt that she was completely calm, I turned her to face me. "I promise you that I'm sorry for the way that I acted. These past few weeks have been tough for me so I've been real touchy about things. Give me a chance to make it up to you. I'd really like to take you out and get to know you.

Will you do that? At least give meeee..." I put my head down thinking about a joke I'd heard on *Wild n' Out.* I loved it when I heard it and always wanted to use it, but I had to figure out a way to do it. It made me laugh so I was positive she would laugh. The laughter would break that tension she had placed between us.

"Give you what?"

"There are 20 alphabets so give me 20 days for us to get to know each other."

"20?" She laughed. "There are 26 letters in the alphabet." She called herself correcting me.

Muttering to myself as if I were saying the letters, I looked at her and said, "You're right. I forgot the U-R-A-Q-T."

"That's only 25. Something is wrong with your counting skills."

"My bad. You can get the D later." She began cheesing hard as hell when I said that. That's exactly what I wanted her to do.

"Damn. What if I want the D now?" she quizzed, walking up on me.

"Shidddd... Let's go," I said. Wrapping my arm around her, I walked her right past the kids as if I were going to leave them.

"I'm just playing and no you weren't just about to leave these babies in here," she chided as she froze in her tracks.

"Naw, I was just fuckin' with you. I'd never be that pressed for pussy. Let's exchange numbers so I can get at you later. I was serious about getting to know you," I expressed.

After exchanging numbers with Majesty, I finished my shopping and headed home. The boys looked extremely tired. Having them out all day did that, so I understood. It didn't take long for us to make it home since the store was around the corner from where we lived. Grabbing both of the boys from their seats and taking them in the apartment, I was shocked to be hit in the nose by the scent of food being cooked. It smelled good but because I knew who was cooking it, I didn't want any. Amara could do pussy pops on a headstand and it wouldn't mean shit to me. She'd fucked up and we were done. There was no going back on that.

Chapter Nine:

Amara

Zion had once again been on good bullshit and I just couldn't deal with this anymore. It's like the more money he made the more he acted like he didn't wanna fuck with me. I started thinking what the fuck was I still here for if he wasn't going to treat me with some respect. I was ready to move in with Majestic, but I knew that wasn't happening since his sister was there and Majestic wasn't ready for Zion to know about us just yet. He wanted Zion to put in a little more work first. See Zion was doing good in such a short time, so Majestic said he was a good asset to his team. Zion finding out about us may make things all bad. I was going to try my hardest to wait until the time was right, but I hated rejection so I didn't know how much longer I could take this.

"So, is this how it's going to be Zion?" I snapped while walking into my bedroom.

Like always he didn't pay me any mind; he just sat there looking at his phone smiling. He had been doing this for the past couple of days and I just couldn't help but to feel just a little jealous. When I heard his work phone going off,

I walked over to grab it off the dresser and threw it right at his ass. Making sure it hit his dumb ass.

"What the fuck you do that for?"

"I knew that would get your attention. I've been talking to you for the past couple of days and you can't seem to get ya ugly ass face out of that damn phone. Who the fuck got you smiling, laughing, and ignoring me? What you got someone new? Is that the reason you holding out on the dick?"

"Amara, I ain't about to play with you today, Ma. Don't worry about what the fuck I'm doing now. When you be leaving up out of here getting cum stains on your clothes and condoms left in ya hot ass pussy, I don't ask no questions, Ma. I just let you do you. Now leave me alone and go tend to my kids. It's about time you start acting like a damn mama. Go feed them some lunch and get them dressed it's already after 12 pm."

"Nigga fuck you!" I yelled while storming out of the room. I made my way to the kitchen and started to get the kids something to eat. Zion thought I was playing with his ass. I was going to find out who the fuck he was talking to. He's depriving me of dick but bitching because I'm getting it somewhere else; the nerve of niggas. After making the kids something to eat, I dressed them both and then laid them down for a nap. By the time I was finished it was well after 3 and Zion was still in the damn house which was a shock to me. His ass was still in his phone texting and smiling and the shit was driving me crazy. I even tried texting and calling Majestic to get my mind off of Zion, but this nigga had the nerve to not be fucking with me either, today. At this point I was so pissed I decided to pull out my rolling tray to roll up. I needed a blunt to calm my black ass down before I went crazy.

******

After I got the boys ready for bed, I decided to lay on the couch to watch TV. Zion was still in the room on his phone, he didn't even eat dinner. The sound of him coming into the living room bought me out of my thoughts. I looked up and he was completely dressed. Not only did he look like he was heading out on some bullshit, the smell of cologne filled my nostrils. I knew right then and there that this nigga wasn't going out on no street shit, so I wondered what he was up to.

Zion was fine as fuck. That was something I couldn't take away from him. He was a little taller than 6'2 and his body was cut all the way up. The nigga was cut to perfection. His body was rock hard because if he didn't do shit else, he stayed working out. Chiseled abs, rock hard chest, toned muscles... You name it and he had it. He had tattoos adorning his chest, back, and arms. Zion was what you would consider a light skinned pretty nigga, but he didn't care about that. He would get down and dirty with the rest of them and I loved that about him. He had these light brown eyes that were mesmerizing as hell. So why the fuck would I cheat on a nigga that looked that fine? Shit, fuckable was one thing but stability was something else. Money over everything was my motto.

"I'm out," Zion said, interrupting me from my thoughts.

"Where are you going?" I asked.

"None of your business. I thought I was a grown ass man." Zion snapped.

"What the fuck is your problem yo? Why are you treating me this way?"

"Oh, so now you worried about how I'm treating you, huh? You don't like that shit, do you? When I was nickel and diming staying out for days to make money to feed you and my kids, you did nothing but complain that I wasn't making shit. You went out fucking off with other men. Now my pockets are rising, and you think I'm supposed to be all in ya face. But I'm good, Ma. The only reason I'm still here is because I'm trying to get my shit straight so my kids will be good. So, please leave me alone Amara. You're free to do what you want with whomever you want, Ma. As soon as I get my shit right, I'm out."

Once he finished saying what he needed to get off his chest. I was furious, I hurried and jumped up and got right in his face.

"Since you got money like that, why are you still here? My kids will be good. You can take ya ass and go to a hotel. I got a better, one stay at your parents' house since you're trying to save money. I wish you stop acting like I need you here to help with these kids Zion. News flash bum ass nigga, who you think be taking care of them when you be out in the streets so called working?" I was so over this shit. I wished Majestic would hurry up and handle what needed to be handled so I wouldn't have to keep pretending with Zion's dumb ass. The sound of Zion laughing caused me to get angrier.

"Girl, you cannot take care of them by yourself. Don't act like I don't get up and feed and dress them before I leave the house. Don't act like when they sick, I don't stay in to care for them. Yeah you here with them while I'm out making money, but most of the time you trying to find somewhere for them to go so you can go get fucked in every hole. So, don't ever talk to me like I don't handle my business, Ma because you already know how I do for mine."

I was so upset I didn't say anything. I let him walk out the door. The minute he jetted off I locked up the apartment, jumped in my car and peeled off in a hurry right behind his dumb ass. I knew he had to be going to see a bitch the way his ass was dressed. I may have not wanted him and vice versa but I was going to give him hell for treating and talking to me the way he had been lately.

Once I noticed that I had caught up with Zion's car, I slowed down and followed him to his destination. I hoped wherever he was going was close by since I left the kids in the house. I knew they were sleep for the night and if Zi woke up crying ZJ would give him his pacey.

Zion was getting off at the Cherry Hill exit. Once we got to the mall parking lot, he made his way around the parking lot until we made it to Capital Grill. Then he got out for the valet to park his car. I hurried and pulled into the first parking spot I saw. I found one that was far back where he couldn't see me, but I could see him. Zion hadn't made his way into the restaurant yet, so I assumed he was waiting for someone. The sound of my phone going off interrupted my stake out. When I looked down and saw it was a text message from Majestic telling me not tonight, it had me real mad now. I powered my phone off and threw it on the passenger seat and put my attention back on Zion.

The sight before me had my head spinning, my blood boiling, and if it wasn't for my kids being home alone, I would have gotten out and acted like a complete donkey. But nope, I just pulled off in defeat. First, I had to deal with her getting in between what me and Majestic had going on and now here goes Majesty's ass with my baby daddy.

Now I knew for sure me and this bitch would never get along.

Chapter Ten:

Majestic

Things had been going well since I put Zion on the team. I loved how he was making moves and claiming his spot. Hell, I hated to say it, but he was doing ten times better than Kade was. I hated that it had come to this and I was going to try my best to make sure Kade kept his shit in order without telling him the youngin' was showing him up.

"You good, handsome?"

"Yeah I'm straight, beautiful. I'm about to head on home, but you know you can stay for the remainder of the day if you would like."

"Thanks Majestic! I really appreciate you coming when I called last night. Shit had been going crazy between Chop and me," Noel explained.

Noel and I had been cool for years. Her and her dude Chop used to work for me until Chop got greedy and wanted to start his own shit, but it wasn't going down in my city. I ran these streets over here, so he made his way across the bridge where his Pops and uncles use to run shit. I heard he was doing alright over there too since his

Pops got arrested on king pin charges. Chop was grimy though, I wouldn't be surprise if he set his own Pops up so he could takeover. That's how much of a snake he was.

"No thanks needed, Ma. I wanted to see you just as much as you wanted to see me," I said, being honest. I didn't really step out on Amara much but sometimes she nagged me so much I needed peace of mind somewhere else. Lately she had been doing the most and I just needed some time away from her. It had only been a week and she was blowing me up like crazy. She told me that Zion had moved out so I made sure to send one of my boys over to give her a card loaded with money so her and the boys would be straight. That wasn't enough for her ass though; she started popping up at the crib. So, I made it my business not to be there.

"How about you let me handle you right quick before you head out," Noel said while standing up and sliding in between my legs. Since I was still sitting on the bed, she pushed me back and climbed on top of me. Noel then started placing soft kisses on me starting, with my forehead, and then cheek to cheek before our lips finally met. After placing kisses all over my face she made her way down to my chest, kissing, licking, and sucking all over me. Before making her way down to my hard ass dick she reached down and gave me a couple of strokes causing my eyes to roll back in my head. When she was finished stroking me, she eased her way down there and now she was face to face with my dick. Noel kissed the tip of my dick before she took me all the way in her warm, wet mouth. I had my eyes up at the ceiling trying not to look at her fine ass.

"Majestic, look at me baby! I want you to watch while I suck the soul out of you," Noel managed to get out between sucks, licks, and slurps. Watching her do my dick the way she was doing it did something to me. Watching her deep throat my shit caused my body to start to shake and my seeds to start shooting down her throat.

"Fuck girl! You still be sucking dick like you in a contest," I said while trying to get my breathing in order.

"Now, you know I have to leave an impression since it may be a long time before I see you again." Noel giggled. I couldn't do shit but laugh. Noel was fine as fuck with a short Halle Berry cut that complemented her slim face. She was kind of tall and what some would call slim thick.

She was tall for a female but shorter than me. She was book and street smart; she was definitely a hustler's wife. If she wasn't Chop's, she would definitely be mine.

"Damn girl, I got shit to do today but all I wanna do is lay up under ya sexy ass."

"You the boss, put somebody else on it and then you can have me for the rest of the day."

Shit, Noel was right. I pulled my phone out and shot Zion a text giving him the rundown so he could handle what I needed done. Then, I shut both phones off and took my ass to sleep while cuddling next to Noel.

****

After napping and fucking Noel all day I decided to take my black ass home, finally. I had woken up to missed calls and text messages from Kade, Amara, and one from Zion telling me that everything was handled. The minute I jumped out of my car and was making my way up my steps the sound of Amara screaming my damn name annoyed me. She tried to come up the walkway, but my security stopped her. I waved my hand giving him the ok to let her in the gate. I sat down on my patio set waiting for her to come up the long walkway. I really didn't wanna deal with her, but I knew she wasn't going to leave me the fuck alone until I talked to her.

"This is what we are doing now, Majestic? We practically can be together now and here you are giving me the cold shoulder."

"Ma, ain't nobody giving you the cold shoulder. I'm a busy man and you knew this already. So, what can I do for you since you coming to my crib being all ghetto and shit?"

"I just want to spend some time with you Majestic, that's all."

I knew what Amara wanted and after fucking Noel all night and day, I didn't want no pussy. I was actually good for a couple of days.

"Alright, Ma. I got you. Let's meet up tomorrow, I'll take you out and we can spend some time together. Find a reliable babysitter because I may want you to spend the night with me."

"Ok, I'll see you later," she said while pulling me in for a hug.

"Alright, Ma, and don't be just popping up over here. You know Zion work for me now and could have been here," I said being truthful. I didn't want him knowing about us just yet. I wanted to continue to wheel him in first. I at least wanted him to think we had just started out when they broke up. I didn't need any fuck ups with us since we did business together. I didn't want no crazy ass beef to form over some pussy.

"It won't happen again, Zaddy," Amara cooed while whispering in my ear.

"Don't start with that Zaddy shit. Get ya ass home and text me later," I said while smacking her on her ass and rushing her away.

"Ouch boy!" she cooed while heading back to her car.

After making sure she was gone, I made my way into my home and headed into my kitchen where I smelled dinner cooking. Just like I suspected, Ms. Rose was setting the table.

"Hello Mr. Majestic! You're just in time for dinner. Ms. JJ said she won't be joining you tonight; she had something to do."

JJ's ass had been dipping out a lot lately and I knew it had to be a nigga involved. I also knew my sister, she would put me down when she felt the time was right. She's a big girl so I had no problem with it. I just hoped for his sake that he treated her right.

"Ok, that's fine. Kade may be coming over so go ahead and set an extra plate for me. I'll be back, I'm going to put on something a little more comfortable," I said, letting Mrs. Rose know what I was doing. I knew once I called Kade he was going to come over wanting to know why the day played out the way it did. So, I knew he would be here for dinner.

Chapter Eleven:

Majesty

Everything about Zion was appealing to me. Every time I looked at him, all I wanted to do was feel him on the inside of me. He was everything I could ever ask for in a man, but I didn't want to put myself out there and be set up for disappointment. I kept thinking in the back of my mind that maybe he wasn't what I was thinking he was. Maybe he was just putting on a show to make me think he was some good guy. He never gave me the full details of what happened between him and his baby's mama, so I didn't know if he was the reason they weren't together or if she was. What if he was a cheater? What if he was a compulsive liar? What if he was out there slangin' that shit with my brother and could land us both in jail? Yeah, I met him with Majestic, but that didn't mean he was doing the same thing Majestic was doing. Did it? I didn't have time for any of that drama in my life. Not while I was trying to finish school and get my life back on track.

"What's good, Ma? What's on your mind?" he asked, removing me from my thoughts.

We'd had a great time at the restaurant and were now back at his place. He told me he'd recently moved in which explained why there were still boxes everywhere. We were supposed to be doing that, "Netflix and Chill" shit, but the way he was looking had me wanting to do that, "Hulu and Hook-up" shit.

"I was just wondering…"

"Wondering what?" he interrupted me.

"First of all, where are your kids?"

"So, we've been out several times and you're just now worried about the kids? Let me find out you only dating me so you can hang out with them." He laughed. I couldn't help but to laugh too. He was somewhat truthful in that thought though. His kids were beautiful and although I'd only seen them the one time, I already adored them.

"Maybe," I replied, wanting to see how he was going to react.

"Fine. Go fuck one of them then," he said. He stood up as if he were waiting for me to get up too.

"What?" I looked up at him like he'd lost his mind.

"You're more worried about them than you are me so go play with them," he chided and pointed towards the door. I stared up at him to see if he was going to crack a smile, but he didn't. I looked around to see if cameras would pop out and tell me I was being *Punk'd*, but they didn't.

"I-I-I-I did-d-d-didn't mean it like that." I was so caught off guard by the way he was acting that I started to stutter.

We both stood there staring at each other. There was nothing but silence between us. It was so quiet you could hear a pin drop. I wanted to say something, but I didn't know what else to say and I didn't want myself to look like an even bigger fool than I'm sure I already looked like.

"Zion say something. I really just wanted to know what was going on with you and their mother. If I would've known that you would've acted like this, I never would've said anything," I explained. Suddenly, Zion fell out laughing. At that point, there wasn't shit funny to me. That nigga was acting all bipolar and shit. Where the hell they do that at?

"I was just fuckin' with you, Ma. Calm down," he told me. I couldn't. I was still shocked at the way he was acting. It wasn't until he started tickling me that I began to loosen up again and enjoy the time that we were spending together.

Five minutes had passed, and Zion was still tickling me. I had to get him to stop or I was going to pee on myself.

"Please stop, I have to use the bathroom."

"Let me let you go. I don't want to have a pissy woman," he joked.

"Where's the restroom?" I asked. He showed me to the restroom and left me to handle my business. When I returned, he was sitting in front of the 70-inch Samsung Smart TV that he had mounted on the wall, looking for something for us to watch.

"You good, Ma?" he questioned when I returned.

"Yes, I'm good," I replied, taking a seat next to him.

Zion turned the TV off and turned to face me. He grabbed my hands and looked me in the eyes with a serious expression on his face. Because I wasn't used to him always being so serious, my nerves got the best of me and I began to tremble a little.

"Calm down," he said. I looked at him, but I continued to tremble. "I'm not about to say anything to hurt you. I just want to be completely honest with you about some things. Is that okay?" he asked. I nodded my head yes. *What was I going to do, tell him no?* I thought to myself.

"I'm listening," I spoke, wanting him to go ahead and tell me whatever he was going to tell me. I didn't want to be left out in limbo.

"I like you, Majesty. I mean I really like you. This ain't no puppy dog shit either. It's been a while since I felt like someone actually cared about me as a person and I enjoy having that feeling. I was with my last girlfriend for three years. She was everything to me, but things started to shift when she got pregnant. We got to experience that poverty shit firsthand being young without good jobs and steady incomes. There were times when we were damn near homeless, but we managed to pull through. Most of that came from the help of my adoptive parents. That's a story for another day.

"After she had ZJ, we struggled bad. We even moved in with my adoptive parents for a few months. She kept clashing with them, so I knew I had to make some moves to start taking care of us. That's when I made the choice to hit the streets. I busted my ass day in and day out trying to make sure we could get a place of our own and that I could provide them with a decent lifestyle. We started to do better and then came Zi. That caused even more problems for us. We needed more money so that meant I had to stay out in the streets longer.

"Long story short, I did my best to take care of her and meet the needs of the boys. It was hard. Yeah, I'm into this street shit but I got into it only to make sure there was food on the table, clothes on our backs, and a roof over our heads. That wasn't good enough for her. She still wanted more. I eventually learned that she was cheating on me. I knew that things had changed between us, but I never knew it was bad enough to make her step out on me. One thing about me, I'm not a cheater. If I don't want you, I'm going to leave. No questions ask. That's why she's over there fighting her demons now. She messed up a good thing and now she can't deal with it. At the end of the day, I always have, and I always will be there for my boys. Maybe we aren't in a good place to co-parent, but they will always be my number one priority."

With my mouth gapped open, I stared at him. There was nothing I could say that would make him feel better for everything he'd just expressed to me and I hated that. He seemed to be such a good man. Even the way he was with the boys had me thinking that they had a strong bond. *How could someone be so stupid to let someone like him go?*

"Does it bother you that I'm in the streets?"

"Huh? Why you ask me that?"

"I saw the way you raised your eyebrows when I was telling you my story. It's fine if that's a problem for you. Like I said, I did what I had to do. Is it something that I plan to do forever? Absolutely not. But it's what's paying the bills and keeping my kids fed right now and that's all that matters to me.

"Truthfully, how long do you plan on doing this?" That was something that I needed to know before I made a decision to stick with him. It wasn't that I didn't understand his hustle, but I also had to worry about my life. This street life wasn't for everybody. There was always competition where someone was aiming to take your spot, betrayal, and other bitches. I knew that women flocked to any man that was taken but when they had money, these hoes be like a whole other breed.

"I really don't know. However long it takes me to stack up the money I need to go legit and leave a legacy for my kids," he honestly spoke.

"I'll give you ten years max and we're walking away," I commented.

"You giving me an ultimatum? How you know you're going to be with me in the next ten years?" he quizzed.

"Just call it a woman's intuition," I replied before our lips connected.

Call me crazy, but there was a strong connection between us. One that I wasn't ready to let go of yet. If I had to stick by him to get him to where he needed to be then that's what I was going to do. With us building together, I knew we'd be able to reach his goal before those ten years. At the end of the day, we were a team, right? If I could stick by Majestic's crazy ass through some of the shit that he's done, I'm sure sticking by Zion would be a piece of cake.

Chapter Twelve:

Zion

Majesty had just opened Pandora's box when she allowed our mouths to meet. I'd been thinking about what she felt like on the inside from the moment I laid eyes on her. Now, I was about to find out and I was more than ready.

Allowing my hands to roam her body, I could feel her stiffen up a bit. I'm not sure if she was scared of me or what, but she was going to have to let that shit go. There was no way I could get down with fuckin' someone that was as stiff as a fuckin' board.

"I'm not going to hurt you. Haven't you been around me long enough to trust me?" I asked, curiously awaiting her answer. She took a little too long to answer for me, so I took it upon myself to move the process right along.

She had on a little ass crop top with some jeans. The way her body was shaped filled her clothes out perfectly. I wasted no time removing her top. She wasn't wearing a bra so her beautifully plumped breast sat there waiting for me. The way her nipples poked out let me know that she was just as turned on as I was. Placing soft kisses on her,

her body shuddered when I took one of her nipples inside my mouth.

Taking my time to give both of her breast attention, I used my hands to undo her pants. It wasn't a problem getting them down because she lifted and wiggled her waist until I'd completely taken her jeans off. The scent of her moisture almost drove me up the wall. Feeling the seat of her panties, I already knew that she was soaking wet and awaiting my entry. Moving her panties to the side, I used my thumb to massage her clitoris. Her breathing increased and the moans escaping her mouth was turning me on even more. I had to taste her. I moved my mouth further down her body. Snatching her panties off, I placed my face in front of hairless pussy and gently placed a kiss on it before allowing my tongue to slither out of my mouth to meet her wet clit.

"Ohhhhh myyyy Goddddd..." Majesty yelled out as she gripped the back of my head. She continuously cried out in pleasure as I insulted her pussy with my tongue. Her legs were trembling as if she were having a seizure. That's how good it was feeling to her. She'd completely lost control of her body movements.

Majesty's juices flowed on my tongue and down the sides of my mouth. Her smell and taste were intoxicating to me. I found myself thinking about what it would be like to have her forever. She was someone I could get used to. That quick, I was addicted to her.

"That feels so good, Zion. Please don't stop," she cried out in pleasure. I devoured Majesty's pussy as if I were on death row eating my last meal. I glanced up and immediately locked eyes with Majesty. Never skipping a beat, I continued to munch away on her plump, wet pussy. The more engaged we became with our eyes still connected, the faster I licked. I felt my dick become rock hard and knew it needed to be freed. Continuing to feast on Majesty, I unfastened my pants and pulled them off. When I'd released my dick, I pushed Majesty all the way down on the couch and climbed on top of her. I kept my eyes trained on hers as I slowly dipped inside of her.

Majesty's eyes rolled to the back of her head the moment I entered her. My thick nine inches instantly filled her up. Once again, her body stiffened. Slowly, I circled my hips as if I were writing my name inside of her pussy, allowing her time to adjust to my size.

"Damn, you tight as fuck," I exclaimed as I grinded inside of her. Majesty was the tightest woman I'd ever been with. Her pussy felt like a pair of vice grips on my dick. If I didn't get her to loosen up, her womb was going to become a daycare for my seeds.

"Yes Zion. Don't stop. Make love to your pussy," Majesty announced. Hearing her say it was my pussy caused me to thrust harder inside of her. I wanted her to say that shit with pride and meaning. Whenever another nigga looked at her, she needed to remember whose pussy this really was. I was not going to leave room for another nigga to come in and fuck my bitch again. "Deeper Zion. Deeper!"

Majesty was taking my dick like a pro once she'd gotten accustomed to how big it was. The way she was shaking, and her eyes were rolling, I knew I was blowing her mind. It was my goal to think of my dick as the best dick she'd ever had in her life. The more I thought about what I wanted to do to her, the deeper I went inside of her. I thrusted so far inside of her that I began to feel her pelvic bone. That caused her to holler out. I was giving her one of the best pleasure pains she'd ever experienced in life. Knowing that caused a smile to creep across my face.

"Take this dick, baby. Show daddy that you want it."

Just then, Majesty pushed me off her and rolled over to her stomach. She placed her face down and her ass up. She grabbed ahold of the couch and braced herself for my entry.

"Ziiiiiooooonnnnn..." she screamed out my name as I entered her. I profusely began pounding in and out of her as I watched her throw her ass back on me. The shyness she once used to show me ceased as she became my very own little porn star. "Fuck baby. I love the way you're fuckin' my pussy. I'm cumin' baby," she announced right before her body began uncontrollably shaking and I could feel her creaming all over me. That was all it took for me.

"Shitttttt, I'm cumin' too," I grunted as I thrusted inside of her for the final time. Instead of pulling out, I filled her with all of my cum.

"Mmmm..." I heard her say as she laid flat on her stomach. I laid next to her. The couch was small as hell, but we didn't complain because we were wrapped up in each other. Then out of nowhere, I noticed she turned her back towards me.

"What's wrong?" I asked because her mood changed as well.

"You didn't let me pleasure you," she whined causing me to laugh. "It's not funny." She rolled over and punched me in the arm.

"Baby, it's okay. You'll have forever to suck daddy's dick," I commented, laughing even harder. That caused her to laugh.

Ring... Ring... Ring...

Our laughter was halted by the sound of my phone ringing. Moving my clothes around, I quickly retrieved it from my pants' pocket. My eyes instantly rolled to the back of my head once I realized that it was Amara calling. Hitting the decline button, I sent her to voicemail so I could refocus my attention on Majesty.

"Everything okay?" Majesty asked.

"Yeah, it's just my baby's mama. I'm sure she don't want sh-"

Ring... Ring... Ring...

Before I could finish my statement, the phone rang again.

"Answer it," Majesty instructed. She sat up on the couch and crossed her arms over her chest.

"Nah. I'm not about to let her say something to ruin my night," I responded.

"Are you worried she may say something that you don't want me to hear."   The fact that she had doubted me pissed me off.   After the truth I'd given her and the moment that we shared, she still didn't completely trust me. That was a problem for me.

"I'm going to answer this phone and when I'm done, you can leave. I don't have time to keep trying to prove myself to someone who clearly is looking for a reason to run away from what we had."

Majesty opened her mouth to speak, but I threw my hand up to shush her. Shaking my head, I went ahead and answered the phone and put it on speaker so she could look stupid when she saw how the conversation went between us.

"Yeah," I answered. I was pissed and it was evident in my tone.

"What you mean yeah? I want to talk to you," Amara stated.

"We don't have shit to talk about unless it pertains to one of my kids," I replied.

"Well, I was calling to let you know that we are on the way to Cooper Hospital because ZJ fell and hurt himself."

"Bitch, why the fuck you didn't tell me that from the jump?"

"You shouldn't have answered the phone being rude," she yelled. "And don't bring no bitch to the hospital around my kids."

Amara continued to yell but I didn't care to hear none of the shit she was talking. I quickly ended the call and jumped up putting my clothes on.

"Let yourself out," I instructed to Majesty.

"Wait. We need to talk about this," she asserted.

"Majesty, I've already told you that once you heard that she and I had nothing going on than there would be nothing further for us to discuss and I meant that. I've done a damn good job trying to gain your trust and prove that I wasn't going to hurt you and it still wasn't enough.

I'm done with it. Now, you clearly heard that something was wrong with one of my kids, so I have to go. If you don't understand that then something is wrong with you."

My intentions were not to hurt Majesty because I knew that she could potentially be the one for me. At the same time, she needed to learn that she was going to have to trust me. I tried the easy way with her, but she was now going to have to learn the hard way. Tough love hurts, but it will be worth it in the end.

Chapter Thirteen:

Amara

I had gotten back home just in time hearing ZJ screaming and crying at the top of his lungs. He had climbed up on a chair to wash Zi's pacey off and fell. I was so glad I had gotten home before the neighbors called the police. ZJ was so loud I heard him as soon as I got out of the car. I left them home often when they were sleep so I felt like it would be fine tonight. This was the first time that something actually happened to one of them. This was the last thing I needed to happen. Now I was going to have to deal with Zion.

"Hello ma'am, I'm doctor Davis. It looks like Zion has a fractured wrist. Since he's such a young age we are going to place a cast on him to keep it safe and to make sure it heals properly. I'm will give you a prescription for Tylenol and some vitamins for Zion."

"Alright doc, and when you finished with the prescriptions we can go?" I asked.

"Yes, as soon as I'm finished."

I couldn't wait until he said we could go. I hated hospitals and I needed to get the hell out of here. The sound of the door opening bought me out of my thoughts and in came Zion.

"Amara, what the hell happened to my son?" he fussed while grabbing Zi from my arms and walking over to the bed to kiss ZJ on the forehead.

"Daddy, I fall down off chair," ZJ said.

"Amara where the hell were you when he was climbing on a chair?"

"Her was gone," ZJ said. I couldn't believe he had ratted me out.

The look Zion had just given me made me think I was only safe because I was in the hospital, but if I was home, he probably would have grabbed my ass up so fast. The sound of the door opening again caused a smirk to pop up on my face since I was saved by the door. I thought it was the doctor coming with the prescriptions, but instead it was a lady with a suit on.

"Hello, are you the parents of Zion Kelly Jr. and Zaire Kelly?"

"Yes, we are, may I ask who you are?" Zion asked.

"I'm Shirley Right from DYFS. We were called a little while ago by your neighbors. They said that there was crying that could be heard from your home and they had seen you pull off. They had every right to believe that you left the boys home alone and they said this hasn't been the first time. This time they actually have you on camera leaving. We also received a call from hospital staff. It is customary that when someone Zion's age comes in with an injury such as a fracture, that we be notified."

I was caught like a deer in headlights and didn't even know what to say. Zion looked at me like he wanted to kick my ass, but he knew he had to keep it cool.

"So, now what Ms. Right?" Zion asked.

"I have to take the kids with me. Unless you have a place for them to go until we find placement for them."

"You're not taking my kids," I said, finally breaking my silence.

"I'm afraid we have to ma'am."

"I'm their father can I take them home with me?" Zion asked.

"Zion you not taking my kids either. I be damned if you have them in some other bitch's face."

"Amara, a bitch is the last thing I'm worried about. I swear you have your priorities all fucked up."

"Sure, since they seem to be close to you and the neighbors had all good things to say about you. I guess your home will be good for them until this all gets figured out. I will have to come inspect your home to make sure it is appropriate before I let them go with you. I'll also have to call my supervisor and the judge to get approval of the placement," Ms. Right stated.

"When will you need to do all of this?"

"It will have to be tonight or I'm going to have to take them with me."

"That's fine. I have no problem with you coming to my crib. I do have to tell you that I'm just now moving in so there are boxes everywhere, but my bed is up and there are no safety hazards," he told her.

"No, he can't just take my kids. I will not let that happen," I yelled out while trying to take Zi out of Zion's arms. I was so hurt and defeated. I needed my kids; without them I would be lonely.

"Ms. Scott, you have to calm down before we have to call security on you," the DYFS worker called me by my last name.

"I don't give a fuck who you call. I'm not leaving here without my damn kids," I yelled once more, this time louder than before causing security and the hospital staff to come in. Security grabbed me and proceeded to show me the way out, but I couldn't leave without hurting Zion in some way.

"They not his kids, Ms. Right. He is not their father. Are you still going to let him take my babies?"

"Amara, what the fuck are you talking about. Girl, don't play with me," Zion said with so much anger and sadness in his eyes.

"Nigga, you heard what I said. They ain't yours. You still wanna take them with you?"

"Amara, I ain't worried about you. You only saying that dumb shit because you mad. These my kids, Ma, so go ahead home what ya hateful ass." The more they pushed me to the door the louder I got. I couldn't believe the nosey ass neighbor Sharlene was all up in my business like that. I couldn't wait to go home and egg that bitches door and spray paint her car windows. Ol' stupid ass bitch.

I knew what I said had hurt Zion, but I didn't give a fuck. I knew my kids were his. I just needed him to hurt like I was hurting at the moment.

******

The sound of Rickie screaming and banging on my door was getting on my last nerve. I knew if I didn't get up to answer the door for her, she would keep banging. I had been in my house lounging around, drinking and getting high. It had been two days since my kids were taken away from me and Zion wouldn't answer any of my calls. I just wanted to see my babies, that's all. I missed them so much that I couldn't stop crying. I knew sometimes I wanted them off my hands, but these last two days without them seemed like it had been forever. I walked over to the door and opened it and then walked away. I really didn't feel like company, but I knew my best friend. Her stubborn ass wasn't leaving until she talked to me.

"I talked to Zion and he told me everything. Amara, how could you? Something far worse could have happened. And is it true that they not his kids?"

"Bitch, now you know they're Zion's kids. I just said that to hurt him like I'm hurting. Now what do you want Rickie? I don't need you here if all you're going to do is judge me."

"I'm definitely not going to judge you but I'ma lay you the fuck out for doing dumb shit. Why would you leave my babies in here alone Amara?"

"None of your business. Now if this is what you came here to do you can leave because I don't wanna hear none of this," I said being truthful. Rickie didn't say shit else, she just got up and made her way out of the door. The last thing I needed was for someone to tell me I fucked up. This was my life and I was going to do whatever I had to do to fix this shit.

Chapter Fourteen:

Majestic

When Noel called me and told me she was in the hospital I hurried over to Philly to pick her up. Word on the streets was that Chop robbed somebody and they came back to retaliate. They beat the shit out of Noel and killed Chop. I felt bad for her, so I had been by her side for a couple of days now. She had to do Chop's funeral arrangements and everything. Even though I knew her heart was with me, I also knew this was a trying time for her.

"Hey sweetheart you good?" I asked while walking into my bedroom. Usually me and her would stay at a hotel, but since she didn't have a man anymore and I was still single myself I didn't mind bringing her to my crib. Her and JJ had been getting along fine and I loved every bit of it.

"Yes, I'm ok and once again I wanna think you for making me feel at home. I really appreciate everything you've done for me this far."

"No thanks needed, Ma. You know I got you," I said causing a smile to creep up on her face.

"Did you see who did this to you?"

"No, they all were wearing mask. I didn't know everything Chop was into. So, I really couldn't tell you anything. I don't need you going after anybody either, so just chill. I'll be alright now that I'm here with you. Now let's talk about the stalker that's been calling your phone all night." She giggled causing me to chuckle.

"That's Amara, her and I had been dealing with each other for a minute. The plan was for us to get together when her and her dude broke up. But he works for me now and I don't wanna mess up what we got going on. So, I haven't mentioned it yet. But now I'm at the point I don't want her ass, so is it even necessary to mention?"

"I mean if you feel like you need to get it off your chest, then do it. If you feel like not saying anything, don't. It's all up to you baby. But, tell me why you don't want her anymore?"

"She started nagging me and wanting me to be up under her all the time. But you know that shit don't work for a street nigga. She not about this life to be by my side while I'm running this shit. I need my calm after the storm. Not a whining nagging ass woman that's spending all my damn money and can't cook."

"What you need a cook for, you got a maid."

"So, what? What if my maid gets sick, how I'm gone eat? Can you cook?" I asked while smiling at her.

"I most definitely can cook. And maybe one day I'll cook your favorite meal."

"All shit! She ready to cook for a nigga," I said while pulling her in for a passionate kiss.

"Where were you when I said I loved you?

And where were you when I cried at night?

Waiting up couldn't sleep without you."

We heard loud singing out front and I ran over to the window. The look before me caused me to shake my head. Amara was singing Keyshia Cole's *I Remember,* and she sounded good and drunk. I knew Zion had the kids because he told me. My man was starting to open up to me and I was glad. Half the shit he told me about Amara was definitely crazy. That kind of turned me off amongst other things. I had no idea she was doing it like that. I knew I was wrong for cheating with her, but not taking care of her kids wasn't right and I wouldn't have been able to do that. My parents were fuck ups and if I ever had kids or step kids, I would make sure they had the world.

"What the hell Majestic," Noel said while laughing.

"I don't know what she's doing here but let's go see," I said while grabbing Noel's hand. By the time we made it downstairs JJ was already out front.

"What the fuck are you doing on my brother's property? Bitch, don't quit ya day job because whoever told you that singing was your calling fucking lied. Now take ya drunk ass home waking all the neighbors and animals with all that fucking noise."

"You mind your business, bitch. I'm here worried about Majestic. You always in our business which is why we are having problems now. Why don't you leave our relationship alone and worry about you and Zion's bum ass?" Hearing Amara say that had me confused. I didn't know what the fuck she was talking about, but I was going to find out later.

"Amara, go ahead home, Ma. You are causing a scene and you know I don't like shit like that."

"NO! I'm not going anywhere until you talk to me. What happened to us Majestic? We were supposed to be in a relationship right now."

"You need to get shit straight with your kids, Amara. A relationship may not be the right thing for you right now since it's messing with you being a mama."

"They not my kids no more. I know you heard ya boy got them. Maybe him and your sister can raise them as one big happy family." After Amara said what she said I could see her looking behind me. Right then and there I realized that she had seen Noel standing behind me. The minute she saw her she charged at her but stumbled and fell her drunk ass right in the doorway causing us all to laugh. I scooped her up over my shoulder and told JJ to follow me. I placed Amara in her car and had JJ follow me to go drop her drunk ass off at home. I couldn't believe she had stooped this low. Amara was going through some shit and I wasn't feeling this shit at all. I wish I would have never got all caught up in her and showed her where my crib was. Now I knew for sure she was going to be a problem. I knew Noel had tough skin though. It was going to take more than Amara to run her away.

A half hour later we had Amara in her apartment on the couch with her door locked. I made sure to shoot her a text so she could know how much of an ass she was acting. Once JJ hopped in my car, I looked at her and started shaking my head. We both laughed at each other before I started the car up.

"So, that's Zion's baby mama?" JJ asked.

"So, Zion is your new boo?" I chuckled.

"Yes, I was going to tell you as soon as we made it official but we still trying to iron some shit out. What about you? Are you going to ever tell him that his baby mama was cheating with you?"

"I don't know what I'm going to do about this situation, but I don't want you to say anything. I just want you to let me handle this."

"It's none of my business, bro. As long as the shit doesn't interfere with my relationship. I really like Zion and I don't want to be lying to him. So, please hurry up and figure out what you gone do. Especially, since this bitch getting all sloppy and shit."

"I know, sis. I got you, I promise. So, what you think about Noel?"

"I like her a lot and I hope you not trying to do her dirty ,she's been through a lot Majestic."

"Nah, I'ma do good by her I promise," I said being honest. My sister and I talked all the way home about her relationship and about Noel and I starting out. It felt good having her there.

Chapter Fifteen:

Zion

These past few months have been hell for me. Being betrayed by the woman I loved did something to me. It had me side eyeing everyone that I came into contact with. Even Majesty's loyalty was questionable at times. One thing I always wondered about was if something were to transpire between Majestic and I, whose back would she have? I wanted to talk to her about it, but I didn't want her to worry or start thinking I was out to get her brother or something.

We were sitting up staring at my now, fully furnished apartment. When it was just me, I didn't care whether the boxes were put up and everything was in place because I was never here enough to worry about things being out of place. Now that I have the boys and have worked my way up under Majestic, I've gotten more free time to be home.

Amara had been blowing me up claiming she wanted to see the boys. That, I had no problems with, but I knew it was going to be an issue when she wanted me to leave them alone with her or let her take them off for a few hours. DYFS told me that I was not to let her be alone with them until they completed their investigation surrounding her and I was not about to do anything to jeopardize that. In fact, I'd actually been avoiding her ass. There was no need for her to see them when she didn't care to be there for them when they were living with her. That was my thought and I was sticking to it. The only reason I was allowing her to see them today was because I really had no choice. We all had to be at the DNA place in an hour to get tested to see if the boys were really mine since Amara tried to be genius and say that they weren't. Yeah, I signed the birth certificate but that didn't mean a thing when it came down to whether the state was going to let me keep them or not. I knew one thing for sure, Amara's ass better not have been telling the truth and allowed me to get attached to these boys and snatch them away from me. That would be the day she took her last breath.

"You okay, baby?" Majesty came prancing out of the back bedroom with Zi on her hip.

"What I tell you about carrying his big ass around? Let him walk because when you not here ain't nobody gonna be toting his lil fat ass," I commented. We both laughed.

"Shut up talking about my baby. He's not fat, he's a little chubby and that's your fault."

"How is that my fault?"

"The minute he cries, you doping him up with a bottle. Let him cry and develop his lungs."

"Shittin' me. He better do that developing shit at somebody else's crib. I don't want to hear all that shit. Then I swear sometimes his ass be going off on me in baby babbling. Let me find out he cussin' my ass out in baby talk." I chuckled.

"Dad-da-da-da bubuna ajeim- shit!" Out of nowhere, Zi started rambling. The only thing I got out of him was shit. I was too busy laughing to pop his little ass.

"You got him like that," I told Majesty before placing a kiss on her cheek. I was so glad that we'd made up. She came to me the day after the shit with ZJ getting hurt and apologized for the way that she'd acted. She told me the reason she acted the way that she did, and I was fine with that. She was cheated on in the past and she didn't want a repeat of it. I could understand that because I felt the same way. Amara really fucked with my heart when I was out there busting my ass for my family only to learn that she was unfaithful. I was glad that I found out before it was too late though. "Where's ZJ?" I asked Majesty.

"He was in the room. You want me to go see what's keeping him?"

"Nah. I'll go. Take your fine ass in the kitchen and fix us something to eat," I   advised her. She looked back at me like I'd lost my mind. I shrugged my shoulders and turned my head to keep from staring into her eyes.

"What would you like for me to cook?" she questioned.

"What's in there?" I replied.

"Hold on… Let me check…" She put Zi down and walked over to the coffee table. She started rumbling through some papers before looking back up at me and beginning to speak. "We've got Popeye's, Burger King, McDonald's…"

"Wait a minute," I cut her off. "Why would you ask me what I want you to cook if you reading off restaurants to me?"

"Because I'm going to cook you something from one of these damn restaurants."

"Huh?" I was so confused.

"When I said I'm going to cook, that means I'm going to go to one of these restaurants and order you some food. Then I'm going to come home, throw a few dishes in the sink and put the food on a plate to make you think I cooked the shit."

"Your ass wild, Ma." I couldn't help but to laugh at her ass. "Let me get ZJ and we can just grab something on our way to the DNA place."

Making my way towards their room, I could hear ZJ crying. I immediately went into father mode and was ready to attack anybody that harmed my baby. Amara included.

"Are you okay?" I asked, pushing his door open and walking towards him. ZJ was sitting on side of the bed with his face in his hands. "What's wrong, buddy?"

"I don't wanna go with her."

"Her? Who is her? Majesty?"

"MAMA," he yelled. I jumped back because I wasn't expecting that from him. He was always a mama's boy so I'd never think he'd do anything that would be against his mother. I'll just assume that he got tired of being let down by her as well, so he decided he no longer wanted to deal with her. Even though he was feeling the way that he was, as a father, it was my job to explore more and make sure nothing happened to my baby to cause him to feel the way that he was feeling.

"Did something else happen that I don't know about?" He shook his head no.   "Then why don't you want to go with her?"

"I wanna stay with you and JJ," he said and started crying.

"ZJ calmed down, son. I didn't say that you were about to go home with your mother. Something was said when we were at the hospital that night that you came to live with me. It's not much I can really tell you about it now because you are too little to understand."

"I think you should go ahead and tell him," Majesty poked her head in the room and said. I looked up at her and thought she'd lost her mind. "I know that he's only 3, but he's very smart. Don't be keeping secrets from them because when they get older, they are going to hold that against you. Let him know what's going on and that may make him feel a little better," she called herself explaining. Although hesitant, I thought about what she said. It made a lot of sense for me to go ahead and tell him the truth. Especially, if it came out that he wasn't mine. At least telling him now would have him prepared for what could happen between us later.

"I don't know about this."

"Think about when your parents kept things from you when you were younger and how you felt. At least explain to him that someone else may be his dad," she said. She called herself trying to whisper but was loud as hell. She should've known that talking to me from the doorway was not going to be an easy task.

"I think I'm going to wait a few more days before I say anything. I really want to know what these results are going to say first. I don't want to end up saying something and it turns out that they are mine. Let's just sweep this under the rug right now," I told her before refocusing my attention on ZJ. "You're not going to stay with your mother. You're only going to see her so stop worrying. Daddy got you. I'll always have you, okay?" I kissed his forehead as he nodded his head up and down. "Good. Now finish getting ready so I can take y'all to get something to eat."

"Is JJ comin'?"

"Yeah, we can bring her no cookin' ass," I replied, chuckling. Majesty picked a pillow up off the bed and hit me in the head with it. ZJ thought it was funny and he picked up a pillow and hit me too. They decided they were going to tag team me and both began hitting me with the pillows. That was cool because I was taller, stronger, and had longer arms, I was about to tear their heads up. We engaged in a pillow fight as Zi ran around the room, in circles, in his own little world. We were having so much fun that we forgot all about eating. Shit, we even forgot about the little appointment we had to make it to. We were having fun and enjoying life. I was not about to let anything steal our joy. At least, that was what I told myself before we heard beating on my door. The person never announced themselves as the police, so I already knew in my mind who the hell it was.

Chapter Sixteen:

Majesty

Amara was really pushing her luck with me. She acted a fool outside of my brother's house and now she was doing it at Zion's house. I may not live with Zion, but he was my man and as long as we were together, she was going to respect my relationship with him.

"I got it," I told Zion.

"Let me handle it. I don't have time for y'all to be arguing," he retorted.

"There will be no arguing. I'm a lady," I stated, sounding like Sheneneh from *Martin*.

"Fine. Handle that then," he stated as if he were giving me permission.

Happily, I sashayed towards the door. I allowed Amara to hit on it a few more times before snatching it open. She was about to kick the door but when I opened it, it made her misstep and she ended up slipping and falling.

"What the fu-" she yelled as she fell.

"May we help you?" I asked her.

"We? Oh, so you live here now?" she quizzed.

"And if I did?"

"Girl, bye! You could never be the woman that I am."

"Sweetie, I don't want to be the woman that you are. I have a man and well…. You don't," I taunted.

"Bitch don't play with me. I'll shut all this shit down," she refuted.

"I'm not about to go back and forth with you. If you were going to do something, you would've done it by now. So, again, may we help you?"

After getting off the floor and using her hand to brush herself off, she tried to push past me and get inside the apartment. I was small, but I wasn't weak at all. I applied all my weight in front of me to keep her from coming in. No matter how she moved and tried to push me out of the way, nothing she did worked.

"Move out of my way," she fussed, stomping her feet.

"I'm not Zion, I don't have to deal with your tantrums. Why are you at my man's house?"

"He's the father of my children and as long as my children are here, then I can be here."

"Well, if you had been the mother that they needed you to be then neither of you would be here. Matter factly, if you would've been the woman you should've been, you would've still had their father. Since you don't, you need to leave and don't be coming around here unannounced like that before we have you arrested for trespassing."

"Zion would never do that to me because he still loves me. He'll never love you the way that he loves me," she boasted.

"Amara, what do you want? You coming over here talking about somebody loves you. No baby girl, I loved you. You ruined that. There's nothing for us to discuss at all. Then you tried to play me and say my seeds weren't mine. You think that's going to make me come back to you?"

"Baby, I messed up and I'm sorry. Why can't we try again?"

"Oh, let me get this straight. So, you had a good man and played over him thinking the nigga you were cheating with was going to make you his. When he started curving your ass, now you want to get the good man back? Fuck outta here with that. Zion belongs to me now and forever."

"Are you going to let her talk to me like that?" She asked Zion as if she thought he were supposed to chastise me for chewing her ass out.

"Talk to you like what? She's simply stating facts. Just leave Amara. You've already caused enough problems. Don't you see how you're destroying the boys," Zion told her, pointing to the boys standing in the corner crying. Amara tried to move past me again to get to them, but I blocked her. There was no way she was going to get in.

"Get out of my way before I move you," she told me.

"Go for it. I'd love to see that happen. I've been wanting to touch you for a while. Go ahead and give me a reason to beat your ass so I can claim self-defense." I was inviting her to the worse ass whooping she was ever going to receive.

Amara got tired of fighting me and did the unthinkable. She bent her head down and bit me on the wrist.

"Aaaarrgggghhh..." I belched out in pain. Before I knew it, I'd sent a three-piece combo to her head. She was staggering like a drunk and blood started dripping from her bottom lip. She grabbed ahold of my hair once she could balance herself and began pulling it. I was screaming because it was actually my hair and the worst feeling in the world was having your hair pulled out by the roots.

Zion sprang into action and fought to pull us apart. When he was able to get us a loose, he turned to face me. He was checking all over my body for any additional marks and bruises.

"We need to call the police," I told him.

"Why? Cause you got your ass beat?" Amara spoke. It was clear that she was delusional.

"Who? You didn't do anything but bite me. I had your ass seeing stars. You wanna try it again?"

"You're just mad because I gave him the one thing you didn't give him and that's those two boys over there."

"That's cool that you gave him those boys. Hopefully the baby I'm carrying is the little girl that he always wanted," I spat.

Without realizing it, I'd revealed to Zion the fact that I was pregnant. I didn't want him to know until I went to the doctor and knew for sure. Yeah, the three home pregnancy tests I took said that I was, but it could've been hormones or anything. I wanted to have a blood test done. I was angry because I allowed Amara to get the best of me and ruin what could've been a special moment for Zion and me.

"Majesty? What did you just say?" Zion's mouth dropped as he peered into my eyes. I could feel the water building up. I was holding back the tears that were threatening to fall. I hated that I said something this way. It made me want to put hands on Amara even more.

While Zion was focusing on me, we took our eyes off Amara. That was the worst thing we could've done.

"Mommy noooooo..." we heard ZJ holler. We turned to see what was going on. All we saw was the back of Amara's head as she ran out the door with Zi in her arms screaming for Zion. Before I knew it, Zion had pulled out the gun that he'd been carrying in the small of his back and ran after her. Silently, I began to pray. All of this was too much for me.   Doing the only thing I could think to do, I picked up my phone and called Majestic because calling the police was out of the question.

Chapter Seventeen:

Majestic:

The sound of my phone ringing brought me out of my thoughts. When I picked up, JJ was on the other end going off telling me about Amara's crazy ass. All I could do was shake my head; this bitch was really bat shit crazy. I couldn't believe that I was once in love with her. Her crazy ways definitely made me fall out of love with her real quick. Months ago, she was out in front of my crib drunk as hell, singing and acting all crazy. Right then and there, I knew I was finished with her coo coo ass. Especially, when Noel came into play. Me and baby girl had been kicking it heavy as fuck and I didn't seem to be worried about anybody else.

"What's going on?" Kade asked.

"Amara back on her bullshit and done ran out the house with Zi. JJ just called me all upset."

"Wow, that girl is hurt. Y'all all done fucked her over and now she losin' it." Kade chuckled.

I looked at this nigga like he lost his damn mind. Ain't nobody fuck Amara over, but herself. When I was her side nigga shit was sweet because I didn't see her on an everyday basis. It was like when we were free to do us, she wanted all my time knowing I was a street nigga. When she was with Zion she complained about the money. Then when it was me, she complained about the time. Amara was just the type of chick you couldn't please at all. She was all about self, fuck whatever you wanted; it was all about her and what she wanted. When she couldn't get her way was when she started her bullshit.

"Nigga you don't know the half of it, so don't go talking about shit you know nothing about," I snapped.

"Yo, you been acting funny as shit since ol' boy started working with us. It's like ya whole attitude done changed and I ain't feeling it. We go back, way back and it's no reason why I should be getting treated differently when a new face come on the scene."

I chuckled while shaking my head, this cat was really jealous of the work Zion was putting in. I knew he wasn't feeling Zion, but I never thought he would be jealous. To be honest, I never paid it any mind 'til Noel bought it to my attention. Then when JJ got with Zion shit got even worse since she wouldn't give Kade no conversation at all.

"Tell me how you really feel my nigga. Let all that shit out, I got time," I said while looking dead in Kade's face.

"I already told you how I feel."

"No, you didn't tell me what it was. You just told me some bullshit. You really jealous of Zion coming in and handling his business, ain't you? Be honest, be a real nigga and tell me how it's fucking with you that he does a better job then you."

"That weird ass dude don't do shit better than me. I don't even know why you like his soft ass working for you. What you gone do if somebody come at y'all with some heat? He doesn't even look like he knows how to shoot a damn gun."

"You sound real dumb, Kade. What are we kids, my boy?"

I was growing tired of his dumb shit, so I was about to cut his visit short and then go talk to JJ. The minute I was about to say something, his phone alerted him that he had a text message.

"I got some shit to go handle, I'll talk to you later," he said while getting up and heading out the door. The shit seemed kind of strange to me, but I didn't say anything since I was about to tell him bye any damn way.

Once he rolled out, I got up and grabbed my phone, gun and car keys and hopped in my ride. I shot Noel a text letting her know I had to go see about JJ and that I would be back as soon as I could. I knew I could get Zi back from Amara, but I still hadn't told Zion about her and I. Especially, since we had been getting real cool. Him and my sister were happy and so were Noel and me. We were like one big happy family and I just didn't wanna mess that shit up over Amara's crazy ass. Not only would I mess shit up with Zion and I, but shit would be all bad for Zion and JJ since she was keeping my secret. I actually was shocked Amara didn't spill the beans yet, but I could see that her only focus was on her kids at the moment. So, she wasn't even paying that shit any mind. Plus, she knew that would really fuck Zion up and shit would probably get harder for her.

After speeding down the highway, I made it to Zion's crib in about fifteen minutes. JJ was standing in the doorway with tears in her eyes. I hurried and parked my car and hopped out. As soon as I reached the door, I pulled her in for a hug.

"Where's Zion and ZJ at?" I asked.

"He went to drop ZJ off at his parents' house, then he's going to go out looking for Amara. I'm scared, Majestic; I hope he don't kill that damn girl when he gets to her. We need him," she said just above a whisper.

I pulled her away from me and gave her the side eye. They were questioning eyes to find out what she meant by "we".

"Yes, I just found out the other day. I was trying to wait for the right time to tell everyone. But since I just blurted it out to Amara, Zion already heard me."

"So, are you ready to be somebody's mama, sis? He already got a lot going on with the two he already has." Before she spoke, she grabbed my hand and lead the way into the apartment. Then we sat on the couch in the living room.

"I know it's going to be new to me, but I'll be good. You already know we didn't have the best parents, so I'm going to do everything in my power to make sure my baby is taken care of properly. I would have preferred it happen later, after I got my career started, but it happened sooner. I'm going to be a mama, Majestic," she emphasized with happiness all in her voice. "As far as Zion goes, he's great with his kids and I know he'll be great with this one. Now, if he doesn't wanna step up, then I'll handle my shit by myself, Majestic. You already know how I am, bro."

JJ was right, she'd always been able to take care of herself. Despite how her mama was, she still managed to come out on top. Not to mention, one day her drawings were going to make her rich. Plus, I'd be here to help with anything she needed me to help with. I knew Zion wass a good dude, but he's also in the streets. Not saying that anything was wrong with that because I was too. I just knew that when and if I ever had kids, I'd probably step back a little and start to do some legit shit.

"Alright, I know you got this. Now, what happened here? Where do you think she took Zi?"

"I don't know, but we were supposed to head to get the paternity test done today. I don't know why her stupid ass would do this."

"I could probably get him back, but you know I still hadn't had the talk with Zion yet," I said, being truthful.

"Majestic, I thought you were going to say something a month ago. What the hell is taking you so long? The fact that I know already is like I'm lying to my man. He's going to be so pissed with me when he finds out I knew. Why are you taking so long to say something? Y'all are cool now, it's no reason why you shouldn't be honest with him. It ain't like y'all still mess around or anything. Or do y'all?"

"Nah, I been left her alone when Noel and I became exclusive."

"So, then what the hell is the problem?"

"I just know shit like this can cause beef and I don't want that. We all are happy and living our best life. I just wanna keep it that way, sis. That's all."

"Well, I think if you say something, he will respect you more. Now go ahead and find Zion and make sure he doesn't kill that girl. If you can tell him when you find him, then just please do, Majestic. "

I guess JJ was right, it was time to tell him this bullshit and whatever happens happens. I kissed my sis on the forehead and made my way out the door to find Zion and help him get Zi back.

Chapter Eighteen:

Amara

I was growing tired of Zion and this bitch playing house what my damn kids. I followed them day and night, watching them laugh and play with my babies. The shit was crazy because when they lived with me, I was always trying to get a break. Now that they were gone, I wanted them back. Truth be told, I just wanted Zion to hurt the way I was hurting. He was my man and here this bitch just pops up and gets everything I wanted. I've seen her hair always done. She'd always be rocking the best shit, and they crib was even hooked up nice. It's like she had the Zion I've always wanted. The one that was making all the money. I was frustrated all over again just thinking about it.

Whaaa…Whaaa…Whaaa…

The sound of Zi crying bought me out of my thoughts. I jumped up and ran to the other side of the room where he was lying and snatched him up.

"Boy, I wish you'd stop all that damn crying," I yelled, causing him to cry even more. The sound of the door opening got my attention. I knew it was nobody but Kade because he was the only person that knew where I was.

"Mara, what the fuck did you do, girl?" he yelled while walking over to me.

"I just couldn't help it, I had to take one of them. I just want Zion to give me my fucking kids, Kade. I don't want him and that bitch raising them. They belong with me and they daddy, not her."

"Amara, I don't know how many times I have to tell you that he doesn't want you. He's where he wanna be. If you just relax and let me take care of you and him, you will have your kids back. Now, go ahead and call him so he can get him back. We need to go on with the plan we already had in the works."

"I don't want anything to happened to him, Kade. All I need is that bitch the fuck out of my way. If you can't help me with that, then I don't need you," I said, being honest.

I could tell by the look he gave me that he wasn't pleased with what I had just said to him, but I was being real. I didn't know what this thing was he had going on against Zion, but I needed his help with getting rid of JJ and that was it. For some reason, I had to keep reminding him that was the reason why he was here with me.

"I know, baby. I got you, I told you I would handle everything. It shouldn't be a problem getting rid of JJ. But while we trying to figure out our next plan, you need to get Zi back with his daddy so we can put this plan in motion. If they get the law involved, you won't get Zion or your kids back. Now call him like I just said."

"Alright, cool. I'll call Zion and have him meet me at the DNA center, so we can get this test done. While I have him away from home you go there and kidnap JJ. I'm sick of you dragging your feet with this plan, so I'm going to help you move faster towards getting it done. This way, with JJ missing, Majestic will be off his square."

I used to have strong feelings for Majestic but since he fucked me over, fuck him! I don't care what the fuck happens to him. He led me on for years just to kick me to the curb for some bitch he used to deal with back in the day.

"Are you sure you wanna open up this can of worms with Majestic?"

"Are you sure you ready to be the big man in charge?" I asked.

"Of course! You already know how I feel about all of this, so why would you even ask?"

"Just making sure we on the same page. I already told Zion that I'm on my way to get the test done. You go do what I said and take her somewhere they won't think to look and send me the address. I'll be there as soon as we get this test done. Kade, don't play with me because you already know I'm crazy and the shit I'm capable of doing when shit ain't going my way won't be good for anybody."

"I got you, baby girl! See, this is why I've always liked you. You one boss ass chick. I don't even know why you never gave me the time I wanted. I would have made sure you had the world, Ma."

Kade had always tried, but nope, I wanted the boss and that's what I got. Now, look at me. Maybe if I would have given him a try, I wouldn't be sitting here tripping over two men that didn't want me. But, then again, who knows? He could be just like them. Plus, Kade was one of them jealous type niggas that want whatever his boys got and the shit ain't cute at all.

"Whatever Kade! I done been told that shit a time or two. Now listen, Zion texted me back and said he gone meet me at the place in ten minutes. Don't forget to hit me back later to give me your location."

I knew meeting Zion at the place to get the test done was the right move because if I would have met his ass somewhere else, he was liable to kick my ass. I even called Rickie to meet me there as well. I needed someone else to be by my side in case Zion was on good bullshit. After calling her and getting her to agree to meet me there, I hung the phone up and made my way to the car with Zi in my arms. I was so grateful he was now sleeping so I wouldn't hear all that crying on my way to my destination.

******

After getting the kids tested and arguing with Zion in the parking lot, I made my way home and sat waiting for Kade to get back to me. But of course, he hadn't yet, and it was late as hell. I laid on my couch looking at the ceiling mad at the world. My life was not going as planned and I was so angry about it. I just needed Kade to come through for me and who knows, maybe after he did what I wanted him to do, I'd let him have this good ass pussy he been trying to get all these years. Plus, since both my men had left me alone, it's been a minute since I had any dick.

My phone ringing brought me out of my thoughts. As soon as I saw Kade's name flash across the screen, a smile crept up on my face. I picked it right up.

"Hey you!"

"Hey, I wanted you to know my plan is in motion, but I won't be able to execute it 'til the morning."

"What you mean the morning?"

"I know you wanted it done tonight, but I had to put some things in order. I was calling to see if you wanted to ride out to the house where I'ma keep her at. It's an hour away and I didn't wanna take the drive alone."

"Ok, come scoop me."

"I'm already out front."

"Ok. Wait, an hour away? I know we ain't coming back tonight, so let me grab an overnight bag. Then I'll be right out." After hanging the phone up I hurried and got up, got my things together, and then headed out to ride with Kade. He wanted to wait 'til the morning to put this plan in motion, but I was sure I could figure out something to have it done right away.

Chapter Nineteen:

Zion

Amara fucked up big time with me when she ran off with Zi on yesterday. I immediately let the people at the DYFS office know what she had done and told them that I was no longer going to allow her ass to have visitation. She'd violated the boys in the worse way. Then she had the nerve to play like her ass didn't do shit wrong when I finally laid eyes on her. I wanted to snap the bitch's neck, but we were in broad daylight so I couldn't. The only reason she was even still alive right now was on the strength of my kids. They weren't fuckin' with her right now, but they may decide when they are older that they want to have a relationship with her no-good ass, and I wasn't going to take that choice away from them. I'll tell you this though, Amara got one more time to pull some dumb shit like this and I'm fuckin' her up.

With the DNA test out the way and Zi back with me where he belonged, it was time for me to handle the situation with Majesty. She slipped to let me know that she was pregnant. I was mad about the way I found out but happy as hell to know she was carrying my seed. I was happier about her being pregnant by me than I was about Amara. At least now, it was being done the right way. It was actually being done with someone who wanted me for me and not for what I could do for them or give them. If shit didn't work out with Majesty and me, she had her brother to fall back on. Not to mention, she was in school going after her dreams. That was the shit Amara should've been on besides some other nigga's dick.

Since I hadn't seen Majesty since everything went down, I figured it would be okay for her to come by. After shooting Majesty a text to meet me at the crib, I grabbed the kids something to eat from McDonald's and headed home. Since Amara knew where I lived, I already knew I was going to have to relocate. I tried my best to keep her from finding out, but she had to have been following me. That was my fault because I let my guard down with her ass and that was something I knew I shouldn't have done with her or anyone else. With the type of business that I was in, I was never safe. I put my life and the lives of those I loved in danger continuously each time I walked out the door. It wasn't an intentional thing, but it came with the job. That's why I knew it was only a matter of time before I walked away from this street shit for good.

Majesty carrying my other seed was just the icing on the cake that sealed the deal for me to know that I couldn't do this shit too much longer. She gave it ten years, but I probably won't give it another ten months.

Zipping in and out of traffic, I made it back to my crib in no time. I checked my surroundings before helping the boys out the car and heading up to my apartment.

"Looks like I made it just in time," I heard Majesty say when we reached the door.

"Yeah, you did." She picked Zi up and pulled him in to her.

"I'm so glad he's okay. Where'd you find him at?"

"Her stupid ass called and told me to meet her at the DNA place. She was doing that shit because she knew it was a public place and I wasn't going to do anything to her. I swear that I want to kill her ass," I expressed.

"ZJ take Zi inside so I can talk to your daddy, okay?" She placed Zi down on his feet and ZJ took his hand, leading him into the apartment as he was instructed.

"I really need to take them their food," I told her. It was taking everything in me not to breakdown. Yeah, I was into the street shit, but I was still human. One of my boys could've gotten hurt and that was fuckin' with me. All because I fucked up and let my guard down.

"It's not your fault," Majesty said out of nowhere. I looked up at her and our eyes connected. Without another word being spoke between us, a lonely tear slipped down my face. Majesty came over and wrapped her arms around me. I dropped everything out of my hand unto the floor and held her. "It's not your fault, Zion. You didn't' know what she was going to do."

"I didn't have to know; I should've been cautious. We all know that Amara's ass ain't got it all and she's capable of doing anything."

"Stop it, Zion! Nobody would've thought that her ass would be stupid enough to put one of her children in harm's way. She wasn't that type of woman. Isn't that what you said?"

"Yeah. I never would've thought that she would do some shit like she did today. What If she would've gotten hit when she was running out the door with him? What if she would've had a car accident when she sped away?

Anything could've fuckin' happened." I was so angry that I pulled away from Majesty and punched the door.

"Calm down, Zion. You're going to wake your neighbors and scare the boys. This isn't your fault. I don't know how many times you want me to say that to you. She doesn't deserve this much of your energy. Yeah, all of that shit could've happened, but it didn't. You didn't know what she could do but you know now. Don't let that shit detour you from being there for your children. They were probably traumatized after that bullshit. Man the fuck up and be the father they need right now! Stop letting this bitch take all of this power from you." I noticed that as Majesty raised her voice, her face squinched up and she began to rub her stomach. That reminded me that she was pregnant. I felt selfish in that moment. There I was, standing there venting to her about the next bitch and not once had I acknowledged her being pregnant or asked her how she was doing.

"You're right and I'm sorry. I can't let that shit fuck with me like that. I need to be there for you and the boys. I'm sorry," I apologized.

"It's okay, baby. I promise you everything is going to be fine," she assured me. I pulled her back in for another hug. I held her like it was going to be the last time I was going to hold her. I didn't know what it was, but something wasn't sitting well with me. I couldn't put my finger on it, but I felt like something bad was about to happen.

Placing a kiss on Majesty's forehead, I picked the food up and headed inside the apartment. ZJ and Zi were sitting on the couch looking crazy. I knew it was because they had to have been hungry. I took them over to the kitchen and sat them at the table. With a couple of paper plates in hand, I neatly placed their food on the plates and sat the plates down in front of them. While they ate, I took that as my chance to talk to Majesty. I wanted to know where her head was at when it came to the possibility of her being pregnant. She had no choice but to keep my seed, but I was going to make her feel that it was an option.

"You ready to talk about this?" I asked her, breaking the silence that was between us.

"Talk about what? No, I don't want to talk about Amara's crazy ass anymore. We have both children, and everyone is healthy. Why can't we just enjoy the night?"

"We can enjoy the night, but it's going to depend on how well you answer these questions for me," I told her.

"What's up?"

"Why didn't you tell me about you being pregnant?" I asked.

"I wanted to really be sure. I wanted to go to the doctor and have a blood test done so I'd really know. I've taken test before and they've come back positive and it was because I had a mass and the hormones from my body gave off a false positive. It happens. This time I really wanted to be sure. Then Amara came over here popping her shit like she was the only woman that would ever be able to give you a child and for some reason, I had to prove her wrong. Even though I know I'm ten times the woman she'll ever be, I still had to throw something in her face. I guess it really bothers me that she was the first person that gave you a child," she admitted.

"Let me tell you something," I said, placing my hands on her shoulders and rubbing them up and down. "I don't care if she would've given me a thousand kids, nothing would compare to the feelings you give me. I'm not saying this for sure, but I do have strong feelings for you and for the first time in my life, I honestly feel like it could be true love. It's true we haven't been together that long but there's something about you that I want in my life forever." I dropped down to one knee.

"Are you asking me to mar-" her speaking stopped when she noticed me tying my shoe.

"Am I asking you what?" I looked up at her.

"I thought you were about to ask me to marry you."

"Girl, you wildin'. I'm just telling you how I feel. I like you but not that damn much," I jokingly commented.

"Oh my God, I'm so embarrassed. I'm sorry! Maybe I should just go," she replied. When I looked at her, it appeared that tears were threatening to fall, and I didn't need that to happen. Not because of me. Not when I was just playing with her.

"Chill out, Ma. I'm just fuckin' with you. One day I am going to ask you to marry me, just not right now. It's not the time and I'm not where I want to be in life. I'm not about to ask you to marry me and I can't give you the life you deserve."

"The life I deserve? I have everything I could ever possibly want and need. What do you think I deserve that I don't already have?"

"So, you think you deserve to be in a marriage with me and I'm out here slangin' that shit? I'm a street nigga. I would never put that on you. I could be arrested at any moment."

"What you're saying is that as long as we are just dating, I can be with you while you're in the streets? What sense does that make?"

"It makes a lot of sense. As my girlfriend, you can walk away from me if I were killed or arrested. As my wife, it's something you'd have to deal with. You'd either be forced to stick with me so you would never have to testify against me, or you'd have to try to divorce me and that won't ever happen."

"Why won't it?"

"For one, I be hittin' you off with this dope ass dick." I walked up on her licking my lips and she playfully punched me in the shoulder. "Aye, you better keep your hands to yourself. You remember the last time your ass tried to wrestle with me. I had you in here speaking in tongues."

"I don't remember, maybe I need a reminder," she seductively spoke.

"Time for bed boys," I loudly announced. If daddy was about to get his dick wet, they needed to be sleep because I planned on fuckin' the shit out of Majesty's ass.

"We eatin'," ZJ told me. My babies were so innocent. I hated to have to put them through the shit they were going through. It was horrific for me to even have to do the DNA tests earlier, but I needed to know the truth. What if something were to happen and they needed blood? Deep down inside, I felt like they were mine. None of that was going to matter until I knew for sure.

Ring... Ring... Ring...

My phone began ringing while I was deep in thought. I was shocked to see that it was Amara's ass. What the hell else could she possibly have to say to me?

"Go ahead and answer it. Maybe it's important," Majesty advised me. I peered up at her like she was crazy.

"Nah. I'm good. We ain't got shit to discuss," I snapped.

"Answer it so she won't keep calling back," she asserted. She was right.   Amara's retarded ass would just keep calling and might be bossy enough to pop back up.   I'd probably kill her ass for real if she did that shit again.

The phone stopped ringing and I was glad. I really didn't have time to be going back and forth with her.

"You looking relieved but you know all she's going to do is call back," Majesty stated before giggling.   Before she could even finish her statement good, the damn phone started ringing again and of course, it was Amara's ass.

"What?" I answered the phone with as much bass in my voice that I could muster up.

"Don't answer the phone like that.   I called because I needed to confess something to you."

"Here we go with the bullshit," I chided.

"I ummm.... I'm going to go now.   We will talk later," Majesty stated.   She appeared to have a look of worry on her face which concerned me.   What the fuck was Amara about to tell me that had Majesty's ass so shook?

Chapter Twenty:

Majesty

My stomach began churning the moment Amara told Zion she had a confession. For some reason, I knew I was about to be busted. She couldn't break us up any other way, so why not tell him about Majestic and the fact that I knew about it? I had to give it to her, the bitch was smart about some of the moves she was making. What she wasn't smart about was the ass beating she was going to get from both myself and Majestic when it was all said and done.

"Where are you going? You're the one who told me to answer the phone."

"I have school tomorrow, so I think I should be going. You can deal with her on your own. I don't need all that stress," I somewhat lied. I really did have class tomorrow, but it had never been an issue for me to stay the night with Zion and the boys before and then get up the next morning and head to class. The more I tried to come up with an excuse to leave, the guiltier I was making myself look.

"Chill out, Ma. You buggin'. Let me hear what the hell she got to say. I might need your support to get through whatever the fuck shit is she claims she's about to confess," he said. With him telling me that he might need me, there was no way I could leave. That definitely wouldn't be a good look.

Taking a seat on the couch, I kept my fingers crossed that Amara would have something else to confess. Surely, she wouldn't want to get on Majestic's bad side. He didn't have kids with her, so it wouldn't be shit for him to take her ass out.

"Okay baby. Let me check on the boys real quick."

"They are fine, baby. Come on and step in the room with me so they don't have to hear this shit. I'm going to keep it on speaker," he told me. I nodded my head and followed him inside the bedroom.

It felt like I was walking a plank. I took my time walking behind Zion. My nerves were all over the place. Amara was on some good bullshit and we all knew it. It seemed like the closer we got to the room, the more knots developed in my stomach. When we were inside the room, Zion shut the door behind us. He took my hand and led me over to the bed. We both took a seat as he pushed the button on his iPhone 12 to turn the volume up so we could both hear what the hell Amara had to say.

"What is it Amara? What could you possibly have to confess to me?"

"I wanted to tell you the truth about everything. I want you to understand why I did what I did."

"Amara, none of this shit matters. You did it and we're done. You did some fucked up shit and messed up what we had. There is no going back and nothing you can say will change the way that I feel about you."

"It may not change the way you feel about me but hopefully you'll be able to forgive me."

"Amara, I have to forgive you in order for me to heal from all of this shit and be able to move on with my life. I can't hoard any bad feelings towards you because every time I see you, it'll make me want to kill you. Just know that from this day forward, I don't want you to say shit else to me. Any communication that we have need to go through the DYFS worker. If you want to see the boys, then it will have to go through them and the courts. I will not ever allow you to get in position to try to kidnap one of them again," he expressed to her.

"I wasn't kidnapping him. I'm his mother. I have every right to be with my children," she yelled.

"You heard what the fuck I said. Matter fact, I'm going to go ahead and get my number changed so you won't be tempted to call me again," he told her.

"What if I want to talk to the boys?"

"Clearly, you don't understand English. Anything that deals with you having contact with the boys need to go through the DYFS workers. I'm done with your trifling ass," he spoke through clenched teeth.

"This why I did what I did. Everything in our relationship was always about you and what you wanted. Yeah, I pushed you to go out there to work for Majestic because I knew you would be a good asset to his team, and you could start stacking major bread. Had I known that you would've became this coldhearted bitch in the process, then I never would've kept putting that pressure on you." That's when Amara decided she was going to be dramatic. She started crying and yelling through the phone. Zion sat the phone down on the bed and stood up. He started pacing back and forth in the room. I'm sure he was taking in everything that she said.

"This is why I didn't want to answer the fuckin' phone. This bitch on straight bullshit with her garbage ass. Hold on..." Zion paused what he was saying and picked the phone back up. He pushed a few buttons and sat the phone back down. When I glanced over at the phone, I noticed that he'd pushed a button to start a recording. He was recording their conversation, but I didn't understand why.

"What are you doing?" I mouthed to him.

"Recording this ditzy bitch. I'm going to use all this shit in court against her," he whispered to me. I smiled at him for thinking so fast on his feet. "None of the shit she has to say will look good to the judge. I bet once they see how she really is, there is no way in hell they'd consider giving the boys back to her." Everything that he said made sense. I nodded my head in agreement with what he was going to do.

"You need to be nice to her. If you keep being mean, she's not going to tell you anything," I advised him.

"I know. I got this. Trust me," he replied, and I sat back and watched him work.

Zion softened his tone with her and began to use a different approach. He baited her ass to tell him about the night she left the boys at home alone and other times she left them without a caregiver. He was so convincing that even I started to believe that his ass cared about the shit she was saying. For once through the whole conversation, the tension that was once in my body was starting to ease. I just knew that I was about to get a little more time before the shit with Amara and Majestic was revealed. That was until Zion's ass asked about Amara saying that the boys weren't his.

"Amara, I really appreciate you being honest with me. It takes a lot for anybody to do that. It makes me think that I can trust you again. At least I want to."

"What's stopping you?"

"You said that the boys weren't mine. Is that a fact or were you really saying that because you were mad at me?"

"Zion, they are yours. I didn't start fuckin' around with Majestic until after ZJ was born and I made sure we used protection each time and that I took a morning after pill when we didn't." It was as if someone had knocked the wind out of me. My breathing increased and sweat formed on my forehead. I was so worried that I didn't know what to do.

"What the fuck did you just say?" Zion interrupted her. His voice raised an octave as he demanded answers.

"I'm telling you that the boys are yours. You should be happy," Amara advised him.

"Amara, shut the fuck up and tell me what the fuck you meant about Majestic. You had me go work with this nigga. The nigga you were fuckin' while we were together? Are you fuckin' stupid?" Instead of Amara responding, she hung the phone up. It took Zion saying Majestic's name for her to realize what the fuck she'd just done. Zion tried calling Amara back a few times. At first, the phone was ringing, and she was sending him to voicemail. It went from the phone ringing to the phone not ringing at all and just going straight to the voicemail. She'd either blocked him or turned her phone off altogether. "Fuck it, I'm going over there."

"Calm down, baby. What are you going to go over there for? If she's not answering the phone you know she's not going to open the door. She's scared," I tried reasoning with him.

"She needs to be scared because when I wrap my hands around that bitch's neck, I'm not letting go until I see her eyes pop the fuck out of her head."

"She's not worth it Zion. It happened, let the shit go."

"Let it go! How the fuck you sound? I'm not letting that shit go. Your brother ain't shit and neither was she. They both foul as fuck. That nigga smiling in my face and fuckin' my bitch behind my back. Then he out in the streets acting like he's a real nigga. He ain't shit."

"Zion, I'm not going to stand here and let you talk about my brother like that. He put you on when nobody else would. You better give him some respect." Even though I knew Majestic was wrong for the shit, I still felt the need to protect him. After all, he was my brother.

"Fuck your brother," he muttered.

"Zion, I'm warning you," I grunted.

"Wait a minute... Did you know about this? You had to have. That's why your ass was trying to run out the door when she said she wanted to be honest with me. You thought she was going to tell on your mufuckin' ass. The whole time you've been in my face acting like you cared about me, you knew your brother was fuckin' me over."

"Zion... I-I-I..." No matter what I wanted to say, nothing would come out.

"You what? You fuckin' knew and didn't tell me. Get the fuck out, Majesty," he roared.

"Please Zion, let me explain. I didn't know about it at first. I just found out. He said he was going to tell you."

"Fuck that! You knew that his ass wasn't going to tell me shit because it wouldn't be good for business. As my woman, you should've told me the moment you found out."

"He's my brother."

"AND I'M YOUR FUCKIN' NIGGA. FUCK YOU MEAN?!?"

"Baby, pleaseeeee..." I pleaded with him. I wanted him to hear me out and understand why I didn't say anything, but he wasn't trying to hear anything I had to say.

"Fuck Amara. Fuck Majestic. AND FUCK YOU! GET THE FUCK OUTTA MY SHIT MAJESTY!!"

"No!" I put my foot down.

"I'M NOT FUCKIN' PLAYING WITH YO ASS, MAJESTY. GET THE FUCK OUTTA MY CRIB BEFORE I DRAG YOU OUT OF THIS BITCH!" he roared a little louder. He was so angry that his eyes had turned bloodshot red, spit was spewing out of his mouth behind every word that he spoke, and veins had popped out of his forehead. I should've been scared, but I wasn't. I was more concerned about losing him than anything else.

"No, I'm not leaving. You're going to talk to me because this shit not right. I didn't do anything wrong. I was trying to give Majestic the time to tell you because this was between y'all. Please understand where I'm coming from," I tried explaining to him. No matter how much I tried to get him to understand where I was coming from, he didn't. All he could think about was the fact that he had been betrayed. I was mad as hell at Amara for doing this shit. That bitch did it on purpose. She knew it would be the one other thing she could do to break Zion and I up. Sad to say that it looked like the shit actually worked.

"FUCK THIS SHIT!" he chided. Zion picked me up, I was kicking and screaming but he didn't care. He carried me out the room and to the front door. The boys saw what was going on and were both crying as well.

"YOU'RE SCARING THE BOYS," I screamed. Zion didn't care. He took my ass on out the door and damn near dropped me trying to put me down. "ZION, DON'T DO THIS!"

"FUCK YOU!" he spat and slammed the door in my face.

With tears streaming down my face, I stood and dusted myself off and made my way down the stairs. I looked like a damn fool and felt like an even bigger fool. Making it all the way down the stairs and to my car, I realized that I'd left my purse with my keys and cell phone in Zion's apartment. As I was about to go back up there, I heard Zion yelling out the window.

"TAKE YO SHIT AND STAY THE FUCK AWAY FROM ME." He tossed my purse out the window and slammed the window shut so I wouldn't have a chance to respond. I knew he was right for feeling the way that he was feeling, but he was wrong for treating me like some riff raff he picked up off the street. One thing I didn't tolerate was disrespect and I was going to be sure to let Majestic know about the shit so he could handle him.   I gathered my things off the ground, got in the car, and sped away.

My mind raced a mile a minute as I thought about what had just transpired. It was wrong for Zion to treat me the way that he was treating me. I had nothing to do with the shit between Amara and Majestic. He was acting like I was the one that put them together. Hell, I'd just gotten to town a few months ago and clearly they'd been fuckin' around for years. How the hell could he not put the shit together that it had nothing to do with me? I was innocent in all of this, yet I was the one that was experiencing the most hurt.

Beeeepppppppp...

Out of nowhere, I heard a car horn honking. I glanced up just in time to see a car slam on brakes in front of me. That caused me to slam on brakes as well. I only missed hitting the car in front of me by an inch.

Bam...

That didn't stop the car that was behind me from hitting me. I looked around to survey my surroundings. There weren't any other cars in sight. I pulled my phone out of my purse so that I could call the police before stepping out to assess the damage.

"What the fuck! You can't drive or some shit?" I yelled to the driver of the white van that had rear ended me. I kicked their bumper when I saw how the back of my car was damn near in my backseat.

With my phone in my hand, I began to dial 9-1-1. My stupid ass forgot just that quick that I needed to continue to watch everything that was going on around me, especially with who my brother was and because I was dating Zion. My eyes were all into my phone when someone came behind me and put something over my nose and mouth. I began kicking trying to get lose. The sound of my screaming was drowned out by the clothe that was covering my mouth. The more energy I was using trying to get away, the more I was draining myself. It wasn't long before I began to get dizzy. Before I knew it, I was knocked out.

Chapter Twenty-One:

Majestic

The sun shining in my bay window broke me from my deep slumber. I looked over to my left and Noel was still sound asleep. My girl was so beautiful and I was happy as shit to be waking up next to her every morning.

"Creep much," the soft sound of her voice broke me from my daze.

"I'ma creep for ya sexy ass," I said while pulling her closer to me.

"Good morning, handsome."

"Good morning, beautiful. You were tossing and turning all night. Are you good?"

"I'm good, baby. You know I'll probably be having nightmares for a minute, but I'll be good."

"What's up with you, though? I've noticed you've been quiet. Are you good?"

"I'm ok, I still haven't figured out a way to tell Zion about Amara and me. I don't want him thinking I was being shady because it truly wasn't nothing like that. I didn't know we were going to become cool. When me and

Amara started out it was only supposed to be straight fucking and that was it until my heart got caught up in her. Then when I started to realize what type of chick she really was, it was too late. Baby girl was already gone and beginning to be a problem. Truth be told, I shouldn't have let the shit go on for so long. Zion is a real cool dude and now I know most of the things I was told about him were all lies because she just wanted me to believe he was some busta ass nigga not taking care of home. So, I just kept on fucking her and giving her whatever she wanted to make her happy."

"You're wrong for keeping it in this long. You're also wrong for putting Majesty in the middle. What do you think is going to happen when he finds out? Although her loyalty lies with you, you put her in a compromising situation, Majestic and I think it's time for you to fix all of this before it gets out of hand."

"Alright baby, I got you. I'ma get this shit taken care of today, but right after you handle him." I smirked while exposing my hard ass dick. A smile crept up on Noel's face and she climbed on top of me making sure our eyes connected. While we gave each other an intense look, we then began to kiss each other passionately. While we were kissing each other hungrily, she was sliding down on my pole causing my eyes to roll up in my head as I enjoyed the warm wet gushy feeling my dick was now witnessing. Noel was now riding me nice and slow just the way I liked. Watching her perfectly B cup breast bounce up and down, I decided to meet her stroke for stroke from the bottom. Once she leaned in a little more, I placed one of her small breasts into my mouth and sucked on it as hard as I could causing Noel to start moving in a faster motion. I didn't know what it was but the minute I sucked on her itty bitty's the shit drove her wild. While continuing to meet her every move, I started to feel her juices running down on my dick as I watch her body began to shake. Not wanting her to lose her motion, I grabbed her waist and held her still until she finished her eruption. Right then and there, I thought to myself, *Got her; one nut down and one more to go.* I had planned to make her cum once more before I got mine.

"Fuck baby," she cooed as she came down from her orgasm. Moving her off of me and lying her on her back, I was prepared to give her a tongue lashing that would have me on her mind all day today.

"Mmm…baby," Noel moaned out in pleasure while I placed kisses all over her pussy before I went all the way in with my tongue.

"You like when I taste you, beautiful?" I beamed, watching her go wild.

"Yes Majestic… Yes… Please baby, I can't take no more. Can you just make me cum?" she yelled out causing me to smile between licks.

"I got you, baby! I got you," I said while slurping, licking, and kissing in a fast motion. I was giving her what she wanted, and I could tell she was enjoying every bit of it. I then eased two fingers into her wet pussy while I continued to lick her juices up. The friction from my fingers moving in a fast motion along with me continuing to attack her clit drove her body into overdrive and caused her to cum long, hard, and good. I laid there and stared at her for a minute, looking at my handy work. I knew she was tired as hell, but my mans was still standing at attention. I maneuvered her on her side, lifted her leg a little, and slid right in her wetness. I moved in and out of her in a slow motion. When the moaning started, I could tell she was back into it. The way the soft moans escaped her mouth sounded so fucking sexy and the shit was doing something to me. It caused me to pick up the pace. Once I started drilling in and out of her in a faster motion shorty began to tighten her pussy on my dick. I wasn't ready to cum yet, but her shit was feeling amazing and I couldn't control myself.

"Fuck, Ma!" I said right before shooting my seeds in her.

After I got my breathing under control. We laid there looking at each other for a couple of minutes and then I helped her up and we both headed to shower together. I smelled cinnamon from my room, so I assumed Ms. Rose already had breakfast cooking. I hoped this morning JJ would attend since it had been a couple of days since I saw her. I knew she was good though since Zion was in the picture.

Chapter Twenty-Two:

Amara

I thought things were looking up for me, but instead, it was like I couldn't get this plan into motion like I wanted to. I thought we were going to just kill JJ, but no, Kade had other plans which made shit go slower than I would have liked it to. I wanted the bitch DEAD and he wanted to do a ransom since he knew Majestic would do anything to get her back. I wasn't feeling his idea, so I was going to keep trying to work my magic on him to get what I wanted. Of course, I could just do it myself, but I didn't want her blood on my hands. I would rather him go down for it.

"Girl, if you keep fucking me like this, I may have to give you the world," Kade said while kissing my forehead.

I had finally given in a couple of days ago and we've been going at it like crazy. I needed to put this shit on him good so I could get shit done the way I wanted.

"Boy, shut up." I giggled while tapping his arm.

"Shit, I'm only telling the truth."

Bang...Bang...Bang...

The sound of JJ kicking the wall in the next room could be heard.

"Kade, please go tie her legs the fuck up so she can stop," I snapped, growing annoyed.

"Man, I ain't going back in there. I've noticed that you keep on sending me in. I know I go in with a mask on and shit, but I don't need her studying my movement so she can make me. You throw a mask on and take your ass in there."

I didn't do shit but look at him like he was crazy and jumped up to go make this bitch shut the fuck up. After throwing some tights and a t shirt on, I grabbed one of Kade's ski mask and threw my big shades on and then entered the room where JJ was being held.

"If you don't stop all that fucking kicking the wall, I'ma cut your fucking feet off. Now, sit here like you got some fucking sense and won't nothing happen to your ugly ass. Besides, we way in the country some fucking where, can't nobody hear you. All you are doing is aggravating me and if you keep it up, you won't make it out of here alive."

JJ looked at me right before she started laughing. I didn't know what the fuck was so funny, but she was making me wanna fuck her up. Growing angry over her actions, I lost it and smacked her right across her face. She stopped laughing and spit the blood out of her mouth.

"Why don't you untie me, you stupid bitch? I bet you won't because I'll beat the dog shit out ya stupid ass. You must don't know who the fuck my brother is, you bum bitch. You and that busta ass nigga that's helping you gone get what's coming to y'all. My man and my bro gone kill you and your fucking family, you dizzy bitch. I hope this all was worth it."

I had so much I wanted to say but couldn't because I didn't wanna blow my cover. I just left the room with an attitude. When I made it back into the bedroom Kade was sitting on the bed smoking a blunt.

"I need you to figure out what the fuck you are going to do with this bitch before I kill her ass," I snapped.

"Yo, you need to chill out. Rushing into shit gone get ya little ass killed. We fucking with a powerful person. You need to relax and let me handle this before you get us both the fuck killed."

I really wasn't trying to hear what he was saying. I wanted this shit taken care of as soon as he could get it done. I was sick of this bitch being in my damn face. I looked at him and started cracking the fuck up. This nigga was really a jealous pussy ass nigga and I was starting to regret working with his dumb ass.

"You really scared of Majestic, huh?" I continued to laugh while shaking my head. He looked at me with so much anger before he jumped up and smacked me so fucking hard, I flew across the room.

"You listen and you listen good. I ain't scared of no fucking body. I'm putting myself in danger helping ya little spoiled ass out, but you wanna do shit ya way and don't even know what the fuck you doing. Doing shit your way, we gone end up dead or in jail. Doing it my way, we could end up with a large lumpsum of money and able to leave the country without getting caught. If you haven't noticed yet, you are never getting your kids or Zion back so you might as well get ya shit together. Soon, we gone have to leave here and if you ain't with me, then you can stay here and die. But until I get what the fuck I want and get the fuck out of dodge, you with me. And if you fuck with me, I'll kill your fucking kids and Zion. Now fuck with me if you want," Kade said, sending chills up my spine. I'd never seen him this way and I didn't wanna ever see it again. I think I was going to make my way home tonight because I didn't want to unleash this monster anymore. Plus, it was time to go home and act normal incase they started snooping around. I knew since JJ and I had beef I may be one of the people they came to talk to.

Chapter Twenty-Three:

Zion

It had been three long days and I wasn't even gone lie and say I wasn't missing Majesty like crazy. I had been lying around and thinking about the argument we had. No matter how mad I was at her I couldn't get her and my seed out of my mind. Majestic even had been calling but I wasn't answering his ass either. The sound of banging on my front door brought me out of my thoughts. Once I jumped up and looked out of the peephole, I saw it was Majestic. I didn't wanna let him in, but I knew we were going to have to talk about this shit sooner or later. I wasn't really mad about Amara. I was more so mad about the loyalty. I'm a loyal person and I would expect for others to be the same way. I thought Majestic and I were forming a friendship. As for Majesty, I loved the shit out of that girl, but I couldn't help but to think about our future. Was I going to have to worry about her lying to me about other shit? Majestic started to bang harder, so I finally decided to open the door.

"What's up?" I said while leaving the door open and allowing him to come in.

"What's good, bro? I wanted to know if you had time to talk?"

"You in here, ain't you?"

"When I say what I say. I want you to know it wasn't no shady shit and I didn't know you were going to be working with me or that we were going to be as cool as we are today."

"How long?" I asked, cutting him off.

He looked at me like he was confused that I already knew what he was talking about.

"Man, what you are talking about?" he curiously asked.

"Come on, Majestic; don't come over here playing with my intelligence, bro. I already know you were fucking Amara. Now answer my question, man."

"A couple of years, but I swear it wasn't no shady shit going on man. I technically left her alone when you started working for me."

"So, why not just tell me from the rip?"

"To be truthful, man, I didn't wanna mess up business. You're one of my best workers right now and the only one I can trust lately since Kade been on some funny shit."

"Yeah whatever, man, and what about JJ? You talked her into lying to me?"

"No, it wasn't like that. I promised her I was going to tell you. Man, please don't fault her for my mistake. All this shit is on me."

"You too late for that. It's already over between us. I put her ass out days ago. I'm surprised she didn't tell you so it could've saved you the trip of coming over here to talk to me."

The look he gave me was strange, so I knew something was wrong.

"Say what?" he asked, scratching the back of his head.

"You heard what I said. I broke it off with her days ago," I repeated.

"Well, where is she because she hasn't been home in three days, to be exact. I thought she was here with you. That was another reason I came over here. I've been calling her like crazy and not getting an answer. This is not like her."

"Are you serious?" I asked in a sad tone. I grabbed my phone off the coffee table and dialed her number. The shit went straight to voicemail. "We have to find her, Majestic. She's pregnant, man," I said, worried.

"I know, man. Put some clothes on and let's go. We gone roll out to the warehouse and call a meeting. I need everyone there and I need people to play the streets close. I need my sister found as soon as possible," Majestic exclaimed with a look of anger on his face.

I ran to the room to throw some clothes on. I was so glad the boys were with my parents. I was going to contact them to let them know I needed them to keep them a little longer. Once I grabbed something to throw on, I couldn't help but to notice the couple of things that Majesty still had on my dresser. Knowing that she was missing had me in my feelings and I wished I wouldn't have kicked her out that day. I felt like a complete asshole and if something happened to her, I wouldn't be able to forgive myself.

******

"I want everyone of y'all combing these streets. If I feel like you not looking as hard as you should be looking, I'ma kidnap your fucking sisters and torcher them. Now play with me if you want. I don't want none of you going home to do shit. I want my sister found and if I don't have any results soon, I'm going to go crazy. Y'all know how that can be," Majestic yelled while his face turned red.

Once he finished his last statement, I signaled the fellas to all leave. I could feel someone looking at me, so I turned and noticed Kade drilling a hole in my face. I never understood why this dude didn't like me. He never said shit to me unless we were working together, but I could just sense a hating ass nigga. Truth be told, I never trusted this fool and I never understood how Majestic did for so many years.

"You ready to roll out, bro?" Majestic asked, bringing me out of my thoughts.

"Yup, let's go."

Majestic and I headed out to his truck and we both jumped in. Kade was now getting into his whip too, but that nigga was still staring at me like he had a damn problem.

"What's with ya boy?" I asked.

"Who are you talking about?"

"Kade's ass! Why this nigga always looking at me like he wanna kill me?" I chuckled.

"That nigga just jealous because me and you cool. He hated how you and I got close quick as hell. He also hated how I started giving you some of his workload. He just salty, that's all."

"Well, he better tread lightly. I may be quiet but I ain't no fucking punk. If he pulling out guns, he'd better kill my ass and I meant that shit."

"You gotta do what you gotta do, man. His ass been moving funny anyway."

No more words were spoken as Majestic and I peeled off with no special location in mind. We just knew we needed to comb these streets to find my girl.

Chapter Twenty-Four:

Majesty

I was tired, starving, and scared. At first, I was ok because I just knew my brother or Zion would've been here to get me by now. But we were on day four and I was still here waiting for someone to come get me. I wasn't sure who these fools were that had me, but I could tell they were getting on each other's nerves. So, I devised a plan to try to turn them against each other. That way, I could get the fuck out of here.

The sound of the door opening brought me out of my thoughts. The guy was coming in with a Popeye's Chicken bag. I was starving too. I would never eat from the chick because she would always bring me food that she cooked. I wasn't going to chance her poisoning me. At least he would always bring me take out. I knew all of this junk wasn't good for the baby, but I also knew that I needed to eat. He sat the bag on the floor but didn't say shit. The smart thing about him was that he wouldn't talk much, and when he did, he would disguise his voice. That made me put two and two together. I either knew this dude or he knew my brother and didn't wanna chance getting caught by me recognizing him.

"Hey, can you stay a while and talk to me for a little bit?" I asked just to see what he would say.

"No, I got shit to do and sitting in here talking to you ain't it. Besides, why you wanna all of a sudden talk to me? I mean why you wanna talk to me?" He hurried and fixed what he had just said while still disguising his voice. What he said made a signal go off in my head. What did he mean by why I all of a sudden wanted to talk to him?

"Well, can you at least untie my hands so I can eat?" I asked.

"I'll let your hands loose so you can eat, but if you try something I'ma kill you and I mean it."

My feet were tied together, there was no way I would be able to try to run for it. So, I had plans on just eating. I was still going to sit here and take in everything about this dude. I needed to try to figure out why they had me here and what they wanted with me.

"You know that girl not gone be loyal to you, right? She is making her own plans without you. We be having girl talk when you not here," I lied.

"Shut the fuck up and eat the damn food before I take the rest of that shit and throw it in the damn trash," he snapped. I knew I hit a nerve when he yelled at me.

"I'm just trying to help you out, playa," I said while putting another piece of chicken in my mouth. I could tell I was pissing him off, but I didn't care. I was just trying to figure out a way to make these two be at each other's throat and then possibly kill each other. Then, I could get the hell out of here. The room was quiet, and I was sure the only thing that could be heard was me chewing the shit out of this food since I hadn't eaten in a couple of days.

"So, tell me what her plan is," he said, shocking the hell out of me.

"Oh, so now you wanna sit and talk with me, huh?"

"TALK!" he said while pointing a gun at me.

At this point, I was shaking scared. I had no clue what to say. I didn't know anything about this girl and I damn sure didn't know what they had going on. That gun being pointed at me had me thinking fast.

"She just told me that this was all your plan and she had nothing to do with it. She begged me to tell whoever saves me that it was all you. If you wanna stay alive, I would do whatever I had to do to get me back with my family because sooner or later, she's going to flip on you," I exaggerated.

From the looks of things, I could tell his blood was boiling. Yet, he didn't say a word. He simply got up, snatched away the food I had in my hands, and tied them back. Then, he walked out the room leaving me there all alone. I wasn't sure if what I did helped me any, but I was going to pray that it did.

Chapter Twenty-Five:

Amara

Kade called me and told me to pop up to the house he was holding Majesty at because he had some shit he needed to tell me. In the back of my mind, I felt like he was going to hit me with some bullshit, and I didn't have time for it. However, I still went because we needed to be on one accord until this shit was over with. Hell, I wanted Majesty dead as fuck, but it made sense for me to try to get some money out the deal since both Majestic and Zion were done fuckin' with me.

"What took you so long?" Kade asked when I walked inside the beat-up ass house.

"I had shit to do. Didn't you say we had to watch all of our movements to not make us look suspect? Damn, chill out," I fussed. I hadn't been there a good five minutes and he was already getting on my fuckin' nerves.

"Whatever. What's all this bullshit this bitch talking about?"

"What bullshit?"

"She said that you supposed to be turning against me. What the fuck she talking about? I already don't trust bitches and the shit she saying making you look guilty as fuck. It sounds like some shit your ass would do too," he fumed.

"I don't know what this bitch told you and I don't care. Don't call me with no dumb shit when I've never given you a reason not to trust me," I snarled.

"You've given me a million and one reasons not to trust your scandalous ass and you know it. You cheated on your nigga then had him go work for the nigga you cheated with him on. Hell, you don't even know who the hell the father of your children are. It don't make no damn sense. I never should've trusted your ass from the jump," he scolded. It pissed me off.

One thing I never liked was for people to judge me. Everything coming out of Kade's mouth was telling me that he was passing judgement on me. Who the hell was he to think he could judge me when he was worse than me? Majestic was supposed to be his best friend. They'd worked together for years and just because Zion came into the picture, Kade decided he wanted to bitch up. There ain't no way in hell I would allow someone to come in and fuck up my money the way that Kade had allowed Zion to do him.

"Come on. We 'bout to go in there and address this bitch right now because I don't have time for this shit," I spat.

Without thinking, I stormed into the room that we were holding Majesty in.

"Listen bitch, I've had more than enough of you to last a lifetime. I'm sick of your ass coming in and destroying everything that has been good in my life. You came between me and both of my men. You think I'm going to let you live after this." I was so busy going off about the way that I was feeling that it hadn't dawned on me that I'd revealed who I was.

"You!" she exclaimed. "I should've known that you had something to do with this. Let me go so I can beat your ass," she grunted. That's when I realized what I'd done.

Turning around, I noticed that Kade was wearing a mask. Seeing that angered me even more because he was clearly looking out for himself and not me. How the hell could he let me be so careless? His ass didn't know that if I went down, I was going to take his dumb ass with me.

"You might as well tell me who your little accomplice is because my brother is coming for both of your asses."

"Your brother not going to do shit. He probably don't even know that your ass is gone right now."

"I'm sure he does. If he doesn't, then I know Zion does. He gets this good pussy every night. You don't think he's going to wonder where I'm at when we didn't fuck that first night? Bitch, he licks every inch of my body because it's the best he ever had. Don't get mad at me because he don't want your dirty pussy no more. You're a fuckin' slut." Majesty was spewing all kinds of shit out of her mouth. She was being reckless and didn't give a damn. It was as if she was in control and we weren't.

"Fuck you," I yelled as I walked up on her. Lifting my foot, I sent it flying into her stomach. She wanted to talk about how she had gotten pregnant by Zion, but I was going to show her that she would never give him a baby. That was my job. He had two, he didn't need anymore. Not by her mud duck ass.

"Amara, what the fuck are you doing? She's pregnant," Kade grabbed me. He dragged me out of the room kicking and screaming.

"Let me go. Fuck that bitch. She will no longer be able to take anything from me."

"She didn't take anything from you. You and Zion were done before she started fuckin' with him."

"I don't care. Had she not been around then I could've gotten him back. She was the reason he finally decided he was going to leave the house that we'd made a home."

"That house wasn't a fuckin' home. You were giving Majestic the pussy and was willing to leave Zion for Majestic. I can't believe you," Kade stated.

"Fuck you mean you can't believe me? When the hell did you all of a sudden get a heart?" I questioned him.

"I've been had a heart. Why the fuck you think I didn't kill her ass? You stupid as fuck, Amara. Then you took your dumb ass in there without a mask. You don't think Majestic is going to find your silly ass?"

"If he finds me then he's going to find you too. So, if I were you, I'd try to keep me safe," I suggested to him.

"I ain't trying to keep you shit. I told your dumb ass about being a hot head. Had you listened to me then you never would've gone in there uncovered. It's only a matter of time before Majestic comes for her because I'm not killing her. When I get my money, I'm getting the fuck out of dodge," he informed me.

"Fuck it. Since you're so ready to give me up then how about I go ahead and tell Majestic what the fuck happened to his beloved sister. When I go to him, he's going to believe me and I'm going to tell him it was all you. He's going to kill you without giving you a chance to explain." An evil smile crept across my face. If push came to shove, that's exactly what I was going to do.

"You think he's going to give a fuck about you confessing to him that I had something to do with her kidnapping? He's going to kill me then he's going to kill your retarded ass too. You're stupider than I thought. So not only is your pussy trash, but so is your fuckin' brain cells because you have to be the dumbest bitch I ever met in my life."

The way he was judging me and talking down on me enraged me. I charged at him without blinking an eye. Wildly swinging and crying out, I hit him wherever I could get my hands to connect on his body. He was going to learn that I was not the bitch to fuck with. This shit hadn't gone the way that I thought it would. Had I known from the jump that he never had any intentions of killing her ass then I would've thought of another way to get rid of her. This whole plan needed to be demolished. If it didn't, Kade was going to get both of our asses killed. My only issue now, was finding a way out of this shit. ALIVE!

"Majestic loves me, so he would never do anything to hurt me. That's more than what I can say about what he would do to you."

"I'm not going to argue with you. If I'm dead, then you are. Whether you want to believe it or not, you are not important to Majestic. He's got a new bitch and he's very happy. You weren't shit to him but a dose of pussy when he didn't feel like lookin' for the next bitch. You never meant a damn thing to him. If you did, then he would've taken your ass in as soon as Zion and you were done. Matter fact, Majestic was the man in these streets. If he really wanted to be with you, he would've taken your ass from Zion a long time ago. I'm not sure what your ignorant ass don't get about that."

"Fuck you, Kade!" I hollered.

"Don't be screaming out my name and trying to get me caught up since your flicted ass went in there and let her see you. That was the stupidest thing you ever could've done. I'll be sure to wear black at your funeral though. Might even sing a hymn," he stated before he cracked up laughing. The shit wasn't funny to me.

Everything that Kade was saying to me was correct. I couldn't have been shit to Majestic because he had everything that I wanted and needed, and not once did he offer for me and the boys to come live with him. He never even mentioned the boys when I would talk about us being together. It was crazy that it took me all this time to see that. The even more fucked-up part was that I'd thrown my whole life away for a nigga that played me for pussy. Now, I was left trying to figure out how I'd be able to get out of this shit alive.

Chapter Twenty-Six:

Majestic

"Baby, you need to get some rest. You have been beating the streets for days looking for Majesty. You won't be any good to her if something were to happen to you," Noel advised me, but I wasn't trying to hear anything she was saying.

"Noel, now is not the time for you to be trying to get me to rest. I can't rest. How can I when my pregnant sister is out there, missing? Who would be ignorant enough to do this shit?"

"I know what can make you relax a little," she said with a smirk on her face. I watched on as Noel licked her lips and then dropped down to her knees before me. It had been days since the last time we pleased each other, and it was really the furthest thing from my mind. But there was no way I could deny her this dick. I wasn't about to start telling her no and she start going somewhere else for it. I knew she'd do it because that's how me and her started fuckin' around. The lack of attention she was getting from Chop mixed with the constant arguing and disrespect also factored into what we had going on. Yeah, I was wrong for fuckin' with her when she had a man, but I wanted her in the worse way.

Come to think of it, the last few chicks I've dealt with, I fucked with them while they had a man. That bothered me because I've always heard people say, "The way you get them is the way you lose them." Even though I didn't want to think about it, I'd go crazy if I were ever to lose Noel.

"Sssss...." I hissed as she swallowed my dick whole. That completely caused me to refocus on what she was doing to me. My body lifted up as if I were trying to get up from where I was sitting but I really wasn't. Noel must've felt my movement because she pushed me back to where my back was on the bed.

With my eyes opened, I stared up at the ceiling enjoying everything that Noel was doing to me. Each time she deep throated my dick, my ass lifted off the bed. It got so bad that I no longer wanted head. I wanted to beat her pussy up.

Pulling her up towards me, I was glad that her ass was already naked. I knew that she got super soaker wet every time she sucked my dick, so it didn't take much for me to sit her down on my dick and wait for her tight pussy to adjust to my size. We'd been together several times, so you'd think she'd be used to my dick by now. But it seemed like her ass was still tensing up each time I wanted her to take it like a champ. That was fine by me because it meant I was doing something right.

"Mmmmm...." she sighed as she rested on my dick.

After a few seconds she began rocking back and forth like she was in a rocking chair. With my hands on her waist, I helped her with her movement. When I felt my nut rising, I held her down and allowed her to grind on me. It took everything in me not to bust. The shit felt immaculate.

"You missed this dick, baby?"

"Hell yeah. Don't ever keep this dick from me again," she said just above a whisper. She pushed down harder and moved her body faster with her grinding. She started winding her hips like she was doing some type of reggae dance.

"Fuckkkkkkk baby... I'm cumin'," I grunted as I pushed her off me. Noel got eye level with my dick and placed it back in her mouth as I coated her throat with my seeds.

After she'd swallowed everything I'd deposited into her mouth, she licked and sucked on my dick a little longer to clean it. I almost lost my shit because my dick was still sensitive, and a sensitive dick was not meant to be sucked on the way that Noel was doing.

Moments later, Noel laid her head on my chest. That should've been a moment that I enjoyed but I couldn't. My mind wandered elsewhere. I couldn't help but to ponder over where Majesty was, who took her, what they could've been doing to her, and if I was going to see her alive again.

"I'm sorry," Noel apologized to me.

"For what?" I quizzed.

"I shouldn't have done that. I really wanted to do something to take your mind off what was going on with your sister," she explained.

"You don't have to apologize. I would've done the same for you. If anything, I'm the one that should be apologizing. I haven't been giving you the time and attention that you need, and I just busted without making sure you got your nut. You know that's not like me at all," I said.

"You have a lot on your mind, so I understand. Besides, this was about you, not me. Just know that I'm here for you no matter what."

"You think I'm worried about you going somewhere? You're my ride or die. Your ass not going anywhere," she gushed with a big cheesy grin plastered on her face.

Knock... Knock... Knock...

Someone knocked on the door before I had a chance to respond to her. It couldn't have been anyone but Rose's ass. Her old ass was probably listening at the door and playing with her old wrinkled ass pussy in the process.

"Sup Rose?" I called out. She knew not to open the door unless I told her to come in.

"Mr. Zion is here to see you, sir," she told me.

"Fuck, I forgot he was coming. Tell him I'll be down in a minute," I told her. "Hop up, baby," I instructed Noel.

"Noooo... I don't want you to go," she whined.

"Come on, girl. You know I wouldn't leave unless I had to."

"I know. Just promise me that you're going to come back to me in one piece."

"I got you, Ma."

While Noel climbed under the covers to take a nap, I hopped in the shower to get the nut and shit off me. Throwing on a pair of basketball shorts and a white tee, I slid my feet in my Nike slides and headed down the stairs to meet Zion. With any luck, he had something good to tell me.

Chapter Twenty-Seven:

Zion

Ever since I learned that Majesty was missing all I could do was blame myself. If I wouldn't have gotten so upset with her and told her to leave, then she would've been at the crib with me and the boys or at least at home with Majestic.

"Sup bro?" Majestic came into his living room and dapped me up.

"I found her car," I told him.

"Found her car? Where the fuck did you find it and where the hell is she?" he roared.

"I know someone that works at the police department. I asked them to be on the lookout for her car. She called me today and told me that Majesty's car was found abandoned not too far from where I live. That means that they grabbed her right after she left my apartment. Fuck!" I punched the wall thinking about the shit because again, it seemed like it was all my fault.

The only thing I could imagine that could've happened to her was that her mind was all over the place worrying about how she was going to apologize to me or get me to talk to her again about the fuck shit that she had kept from me. With her thoughts being unclear, that left room for someone to come in and snatch her or do something to hurt her because she would not be watching her back. None of the shit with Amara and Majestic was her fault. She didn't deserve for me to take my anger out on her like that.

"What happened between you two?" Majestic asked me.

"What you mean? I told you I made her leave because she was keeping shit from me?"

"It's funny how nobody else has been able to find out anything about Majesty but your ass comes in here today talking about you found her car and it was close to your crib. Did you do something to my sister?" Majestic was suddenly amped up. If he knew like I did, he'd better pipe the fuck down before I knocked snot out of his nostrils.

"Nigga, are you out of your fuckin' mind? Why the fuck would I do anything to hurt Majesty?" I raised my voice higher than his to challenge his ass. I was not going to back down just because he was a big, burly ass lookin' nigga.

"To get back at me for fuckin' Amara's ugly ass." I couldn't help but laugh. Now, Amara was ugly, but I bet he wasn't saying none of that shit when he was fuckin' her. "What the fuck is so funny?" he quizzed.

"The fact that you would accuse me of doing something to Majesty is throwing me for a loop. I found out Amara's ass was cheating on me, so I let that bitch go and she's the mother of my kids. Then, she told me that my kids might not fuckin' even be mine. If I wanted to kill or hurt anybody, it would be her mufuckin' ass," I told him.

"I'm not trying to hear none of that shit. Run down to me everything that happened when you got into it with Majesty. I find it hard to believe that you learned about me fuckin' with your bitch and now all of a sudden, my sister is missing. That shit don't sit well with me. Then you just so happen to know somebody at the police department that found her car. Fuck outta here. You must think I'm dumb or some shit."

"I don't owe you a fuckin' explanation because I didn't do shit. But if it's going to get us back on the same page so we can find Majesty, then I'll tell you again what the fuck happened. Amara called me on some bullshit and let it slide that you and her had been fuckin' around. Majesty was acting suspect as hell, so I asked her if she knew about you and Amara. She tried to explain herself to me and why she didn't tell me about the shit but I didn't want to hear it. I told her to get the fuck out. I tossed her ass the fuck out of here."

"Fuck you mean you tossed her out? You put your hands on my sister?" He walked up on me.

"I picked her ass up and walked her the fuck out the door. When she got out the door, I tossed her fuckin' purse out the window to her ass. I didn't want to say shit to her or see her from that day forward. She got in her shit and left. If you don't believe me, you can look at my Ring doorbell and you can see for yourself that she left, and I haven't had anything else to do with her. Now, I suggest you back the fuck up out of my face because I don't have the patience for this shit. I may not have all the pull you got but I'm not no bitch either."

"Handle his mufuckin' ass," Kade came in out of nowhere and stated.

"You been waiting for some shit like this to happen, huh?" I addressed him.

"Hell yeah. I've been waiting for him to see how yo ass ain't no good. Had Majesty been with me then no shit like this would've happened. I would've known how to take care of her."

"Oh, now I see why you've been eyeballing the fuck out of me. You've been mad at the fact that I came in and handled business and worked my way up the ladder with Majestic.   Not only that, but I won Majesty over; something your weak ass could never do," I boasted.

"Nigga, fuck you," he roared.

"Nah. I'll leave that to Majesty. You not my cup of tea," I taunted him.

"Chill out with that bullshit in here. I'm worried about my sister and y'all niggas trying to see who got the biggest dick. When we find Majesty, I'll let her be the judge of that," Majestic stated. That shit rubbed me the wrong way. I wanted to say something, but he was right. We needed to focus on Majesty and her whereabouts with my seed. I'd check his ass about that disrespectful ass comment later.

"I'm sick of this nigga. Can't you pay this money to get Majesty back so I can be away from this nigga," Kade commented. Both Majestic and I looked at each other.

"Money? What money?" I quizzed, trying to figure out what the fuck his punk ass was talking about.

"Kade, gone back out there. Call a meeting at the warehouse. Have everyone come there in an hour," Majestic instructed him. Kade didn't say another word. He gave me one more look over before he left out the house.

"You heard what the fuck I heard?" Majestic asked me.

"Yeah. But did you see the scratches on that nigga? His ass knows something," I chided. "That muthafucka knows where Majesty and my seed are. You can't pay me to believe that he doesn't."

"I'm with you on that. Don't worry, I'm on it. His ass is going to call a meeting, but I bet he makes some stops in between. I'm going to get my guy to bug his phone and have some of the other guys trail his ass. He already slipped up with that comment so you know his ass will slip up again."

"What are we supposed to do until then?"

"We have to wait his ass out. He's not going to kill her because he knows that's a definite death wish. But I'm going to kill his ass either way. That muthafucka is about to demand money from me. Watch what I tell you. When he does, it's a wrap."

"What you mean? You not going to give him the money to save Majesty?" I was curious as to what he would say. If I had the money, I'd give it all away to bring her back. She was worth my life to be honest. It was sad that it took all of this shit to happen for me to realize that.   I really was in love with her.

"I'm going to give him the money but I'm going to have a tracking device on that money so wherever he goes, I'll be right there to meet his ass. I'm sure he didn't' do this shit alone either. It's only a matter of time before we get to the bottom of this shit." Majestic was too calm for me. I knew the nigga was crazy and killing people wasn't shit to him so why was he so calm? Majesty was still missing. Was it worth allowing Kade to continue acting as if he didn't know where she was?

"I don't know about this shit. It seems too fuckin' risky. I don't want anything to happen to Majesty."

"She's going to be okay, Zion. One thing that I know about Kade is that he is in love with Majesty. He's not going to let anything happen to her. His ass got jealous and found a way to get money out of me because his pockets began to dry up when you hit the scene. Watch what I tell you. I'm going to let this shit play out. I can promise you that we will have Majesty back home safely within the next few days. Watch what I tell you."

Majestic was so sure of himself, but my ass was still worried. My nerves were all over the place. My body was shaking like a hoe in church. I needed answers. I needed to know where my baby was. I loved Majesty and I wanted to be able to tell her that. None of this shit should've happened. Once she was back in my arms, there was no way in hell I was ever going to let her go again.

Chapter Twenty-Eight:

Majestic

"Yo, your parents are mad cool. I used to wish Majesty and I had loving people that would take us in and raise us together, but it didn't happen that way. She got raised with her grandma while I got lost in the streets. I practically raised my damn self, which caused me to turn to the streets at an early age. For years, I used to blame Majesty's mama for my pops leaving me and my mama. But hell, they all were fucked up parents. It took me growing up to understand that. Now, I would move earth for my baby sister," I said, being honest. All this talking about Majesty had me in my feelings and I swear to God if anything happened to her, I was going to paint this fucking city red and I meant that shit.

"Daddy!" ZJ yelled while jumping on Zion's lap with Zi following closely behind him. I couldn't even lie, these were two handsome little fellas and I hoped one day soon, I could calm down a little from this street shit and start my own family.

"Were you scared when you first found out you were going to be a parent?" I questioned Zion.

"A little. I was really just worried that I would let them down since I wasn't financially stable. But where I lacked financially, I made sure I made up with loving them. They mean the world to me and if it comes back that either of them isn't mine, I'ma kill Amara's ass."

"I've been thinking about this shit ever since you said you were getting tested. Man, what if they not yours? What if they mine?" Zion looked at me as if I had two heads, but it was the truth. What if these were my damn kids? Of course, it would be a fucked-up situation and that would mean Amara had played us both.

"Well, I don't wanna think about that shit at all," Zion said.

The sound of Zion's mama calling him halted our conversation.

"Mama, I'm in the TV room," he yelled back.

"Hey baby, sorry to interrupt you, but the mail man just handed me this," she said, while handing him a big yellow envelope. He took it from her, and she left the room.

"Is that what I think is?" I asked.

"Yeah, this is it. That shit crazy because we were just talking about this shit," he replied.

"Well, you ready to open it?"

"Nigga, don't rush me." Zion chuckled.

I knew deep down inside that what I had just told him had him in his feelings. Truth be told, I didn't even know why I said anything in the first place. I should've just kept my feelings to myself. Zion looked at the envelope, then at his boys , and then back to the envelope once more. The room was quiet as shit and no matter how much I wanted to say something I just remained quiet because I didn't wanna ruin the mood.

Zion finally ripped the envelope opened and looked at the papers that were inside. The look on his face told me that something was wrong. Next thing I knew, he picked both the boys up and walked out of the room. When I picked up the paper it hurt me to my heart to see that neither of the boys were his. The shit fucked me up because that would mean they were mine. I got up and headed to find where Zion was. When I made it to the living room his mama pointed to the door.

Outside, the site before me caused my heart to break. Zion was pacing the yard with both the boys in his arms crying his heart out. I didn't wanna piss him off, but I needed to know if they were mine.

"I'm sorry this happened to you.". I called myself being empathetic to what he was going through.

"Are you really? My nigga is you really?" Zion yelled.

"I told you before, man, I wasn't on no shady shit. I swear I had no clue that it was a chance of the boys even being mine because she never said anything."

"Yeah, whatever. I'm not about to sit here and have this conversation with you at the moment. I'm going back in here and give my mama the kids and then I'm going to go find her hoe ass."

"Alright, that's fair. You don't have to talk to me. But I would love to call my friend over here so I can get the boys tested. I just want to make sure they mine. I'd rather get it done right now. Well, at least before Amara knows, if that's ok with you."

"Do what the fuck you want to do. Whoever it is, they have an hour to get here. If they not here within an hour they might as well don't come, and you can get this shit done on your own time," Zion snapped.

I understood his anger, so I was going to let him get his shit off. Once he walked away, I pulled my phone out to call some chick name Angie that I used to fuck with. I knew she was just the person to get this test done and get it back to me quickly. I didn't care the cost because I didn't wanna wait as long as Zion waited. I needed to know this as soon as possible. As soon as I was about to dial her number my phone wrong.

"Yo!" I quickly answered.

"Bossman, we got eyes on Kade right now. He been in this spot for hours now. I don't think he is coming out just yet because I saw some chick just go in too. Shit looks suspect as hell. I think you should come check it out since we about an hour away from the city."

"Alright, and if that nigga tries to bounce, shoot him in the arm or leg and drag his ass back in the house. I want him the fuck alive because if my sister ain't there I have a feeling his bitch ass knows exactly where she is."

After I hung the phone up, I hurried in the house to tell Zion what I'd just found out. He was sitting in a chair looking at the wall and holding the boys. I really felt like shit, but we had other shit to do.

"Man, I know you in a fucked-up place right now, but I just got a call telling me that they got a lead on Kade. We need to go now because it's an hour away. I'll handle that other shit when we get back."

"Mama!" Zion yelled out for his mom.

"Yes, baby."

"I have to make a run, can you please keep the boys again? If Amara comes here call the cops on her ass. She is not allowed to take the boys until I make sure they will be in a safe environment."

"Alright, your dad will be home from work soon and you know he don't play with that girl. I love you and you both be safe," his mama said causing a smile to creep up on my face.

After Zion kissed the boys, we both headed out the house, hopped in my truck, and zoomed off.

Chapter Twenty-Nine:

Amara

I was still in a fucked-up mood and I was ready for Kade to handle this, but he seemed to be getting soft. Every time I would mention it his ass would hit me and yell. I was sick of him putting his hands on me, but truth be told, we needed each other. My account that Majestic was putting money in was completely empty and Zion wasn't sending money since he had the boys. I knew those paternity test results should've been back by now, but I hadn't been home.

At first, I was joking about Zion not being their father. Then, after a while, I was thinking it was definitely a chance of Majestic being Zi's daddy. I knew for sure Zion was ZJ's.

The sound of banging on the wall removed me from my thoughts. *Here goes this bitch starting her shit*, I thought to myself as I walked over to the door and flung it opened.

"What the fuck are you banging for?" I snapped.

"I'm in pain, I need to go to the doctor," JJ said just above a whisper.

"Girl, you ain't going a damn place, so suck it up. If your ass wasn't being smart you wouldn't be hurting right now. I wonder what's taking your brother and my man so long to come get you. I guess you're not as loved as you thought."

"You're are truly crazy. You went through all of this for what? You still not gone have a man and nine times out of ten you gone lose your kids too. Do you really love them?"

Once again JJ was talking shit and it was getting under my skin. She angered me because most of the shit she was talking was the truth and that shit hurt like hell.

"See, this is the reason you're in pain now because you never keep your fucking mouth shut. I guess my partner got some real feelings for you because ya ass still breathing. If it was up to me, ya ass would have been dead and buried right out in this back yard." The sound of the front door opening caught my attention and JJ was saved by the noise because I was ready to hit her dumb ass again. Instead, I turned around and made my way into the living room. When I made it, Kade was pacing the floor and looking out of the window like someone was after him which had me alarmed.

"What the fuck is your problem?" I asked.

"I think they made me. I'm not sure though."

"WHAT THE FUCK YOU MEAN?" I yelled.

"Look girl, you better calm the fuck down and watch who you are yelling at."

"Well, Kade, explain to me what the fuck you are talking about."

"BITCH! What the hell did I tell you about saying my damn name?"

"Nigga, the hell with all that. If you think they made us then why the fuck are we still here? Let's grab JJ and get the fuck out of here."

"Let's leave her and get the fuck out of here. Moving with her is going to slow us down."

"Nigga, is you tripping? We are not leaving her. She is how we supposed to get our money."

"Amara, this shit is over, Ma. The shit went all wrong. Now, you either with me or you not."

That was easy for him to say. They still really weren't sure that he was involved. But for me, I was as good as caught because JJ knew it was me. I didn't care what the fuck Kade said, we weren't leaving JJ here. I ran over to the couch and grabbed my purse. I pulled my gun out and walked into the room where JJ was.

"Amara, what the fuck is you doing with that gun, Ma?" Kade said while running in the room after me. I leaned down and untied JJ's feet, but I left her hands tied.

"Do you think you can walk?" I asked.

"Yes, but I'm in a lot of pain. I need to go to the hospital, bitch," she managed to get out.

I wanted to kill her, but I didn't. I just helped her up and pulled her towards the door.

"Ok, so we going to get in the car and if you try some bullshit I'ma blow your fucking head off. You should know I'm not playing since I don't have anything to live for."

"Kade, we are getting the fuck out of here Do you have somewhere else we can go?"

He didn't look pleased with my decision, but he knew I would kill her fucking ass and for some reason I believe he really loved her even though she would never give him no play. Hell, I wish she would have picked him over Zion and then I wouldn't even be going through this.

"No, not right off hand, but I guess we could get a hotel room somewhere further out."

"Ok, cool. Well, let's get the fuck out of here. We are an hour away so if they caught on, it's still going to take them a minute to get here. Was anyone following you?"

"No, I don't think so." Hearing him say that pissed me off, but I didn't say anything. I headed toward the front door with my gun at the back of JJ's head.

"Remember if either of you try anything, you're dead." I let JJ know before we headed out of the door.

Once we made it out of the door my eyes lit up as big as saucers when a bunch of cars pulled up. I had never shot anybody before, but I was ready if any of them niggas jumped bad. When Majestic saw the gun pointed at his sister's head, the look he gave me told me that he was scared. I ain't never seen a hood ass nigga like him scared.

"Majestic, tell your goons to put they weapons down and let me and Kade go, or you can kiss your pretty little JJ goodbye. How would you like it, boo?"

Majestic looked at me, looked at Zion, and then looked at me again.

"What? You don't know how to handle your crew anymore? Zion go ahead and let him know I mean business. I know you don't want to lose your girl and your baby." I could tell by the way he was biting the inside of his jaw that he wanted to kill me, but he kept his cool since he was in a compromising position.

"Everybody put your guns down. I swear Amara if something happens to my sister you and your boy Kade are dead and I mean that shit. DEAD!" Majestic yelled once more. I wasn't paying his ass any mind. I hurried and signaled Kade to help JJ in the car while my gun was still facing her. I wasn't playing with them; any sudden moves and she would be dead.

After we hopped into the car, Kade sped off while other cars sped behind us.

"What the fuck were you thinking, Ma? You think they really going to let us go with her. NO! They gone follow us anywhere we decide to go. I told you we should have just left her ass and get out, but no, you wanted to argue with me about it instead of us just leaving. If we would have just left things would have bee-"

"Would have been what? Nigga, we had already been done when we were back at the house. Just drive this muthafucka and shut the hell up."

"I'm sick of you and your fuckin' mouth. I say let her the fuck out and we keep it moving. As long as we got her, it's going to slow us the fuck down. If we stop and let her out, we can roll."

"You sound so fuckin' stupid. If we stop and let her out, they gone kill us you fucking dummy. Just drive this bitch."

"Chill out with the name calling, Ma. Look, there goes a sign that says police station ahead. We can let her out of the car there and then hurry and speed off. You know them niggas don't do police stations so they either gone stop before hand or speed right past it. We just gone have to sit still for a minute until we notice they are riding off." At first, I didn't wanna listen to what he was saying, but then I thought about it. It was a good idea because street dudes damn sure stayed away from police stations. I looked over at JJ and she wasn't looking too good. She looked like she was weak and about to faint.

"Hey, are you ok?" I asked, not really giving a fuck. But I needed to know.

"What's wrong with her? Check her pulse," Kade instructed while looking into the rearview mirror and still speeding. I went to check her pulse and noticed there was blood in her crouch area.

"OH MY GOD!" I yelled, noticing how much blood there was.

"What's wrong? What did you do?" Kade asked just like I knew he would. *Why the fuck was everybody so in love with JJ?* I thought to myself.

"Just hurry up and get her to the police station so we can get her out of here," I said while shaking my head. I wanted something bad to happen to her, but now that something actually was, I didn't know how to feel. Then again, that's what the fuck she got for fucking with the wrong bitch's man.

"There goes the police station. Look behind us, them niggas stopped. When I pull up to the police station you have to hurry up and push her out of the car so we can go."

"Just hurry up and pull up."

Before we even made it up to the front of the police station, I had the door open. The minute Kade yelled go, I pushed JJ out of the car and hurried and shut the door. Once the door was closed Kade jetted off. I had no idea what our next destination was, but I hoped to God we made it there. When and if we did, we had to hurry up and make some plans because we both had a bounty on our heads.

To Be Continued ...

* 9 7 9 8 5 7 3 8 4 6 7 9 8 *